William A. Brockington

Elements of Prose

William A. Brockington

Elements of Prose

ISBN/EAN: 9783337368012

Printed in Europe, USA, Canada, Australia, Japan

Cover: Foto ©Andreas Hilbeck / pixelio.de

More available books at **www.hansebooks.com**

ELEMENTS OF PROSE

BY

W. A. BROCKINGTON, M.A.

Principal of Victoria Institute, Worcester;
Lecturer on English Literature to the Cambridge University Extension;
Assistant-Examiner in English to the University of London;
Formerly Lecturer on English Language and Literature in the Mason University College.

LONDON
BLACKIE & SON, Limited, 50 OLD BAILEY, E.C.
GLASGOW AND DUBLIN
1899

"We plead for no system of minute technical rules; still less for the formal application of any system whatever. But to imbue the mind with great general principles, leaving them to operate imperceptibly upon the formation of habit, and to suggest without distinct consciousness of their presence the lesson which the occasion demands—is a very different thing, and is all we contend for." [*Edin. Rev.*, Oct. 1840.]

PREFACE.

Everyone who intends to practise the art of prose should devote some time to the study of method. The student, who has conscientiously investigated but a single paragraph of acknowledged literature, has made appreciable progress in this study; for *method* is to be found only by observation of the actual phenomena of writing. He will, however, in his research, economise both time and effort, if he knows what to look for.

All, therefore, who read in order to write, should first comprehend clearly the laws which all must observe, and the liberties which all are allowed, in the province of writing; though, in regard to the laws of writing, it should be remembered, that a knowledge of them becomes really valuable, only when it has been informed by experience of the actual practice of authors.

These laws of writing bear chiefly upon the mechanical parts of prose; which parts alone come really within the scope of a manual of prose-composition. Upon grace, simplicity, energy, and harmony, we may moralize; inspiration, moral stimulus, here counts for so much more than instruction: the structure of the sentence, the disposition of the paragraph, the right use of figures, we may teach. Accordingly, except in the preliminary chapter of this book, I have confined myself strictly to the *mechanism* of prose. Any mechanism, however subtle and complicated, may be examined in all its parts, one by one.

I desire gratefully to acknowledge the assistance I have received in revising the proofs, from a distinguished past-pupil, Miss Ethel Corbett, B.A., and from my brother, the Rev. A. Allen Brockington, M.A.

W. A. B.

WORCESTER,
March 11, 1899.

CONTENTS.

                                                         Page

PREFACE   ·   ·   ·   ·   ·   ·   ·   ·   ·   ·   iii

CHAPTER I.

ON WRITING IN GENERAL.

Reflective Reading—Necessity of Rules—Knowledge of Words
—*Tautology*—*Pleonasm*—Exactness in Speech—Simplicity
—Clearness—Harmony—A Last Word ·   ·   ·   ·   7

CHAPTER II.

THE SENTENCE.

SENTENCE-UNITY: A Single Proposition; *Subordinate Clauses*;
Co-ordinate Elements; Blair's Rules—SENTENCE-STRUCTURE:
Fixed Order; *Adverb* and *Adverb-phrase*; *Adverb-clause*;
Inversion; *Relative Words and Clauses*; Rapidity of Style
—USE OF STOPS—NATURE OF SENTENCES: Sentence-
Length; Sentence-Resolution; Loose and Periodic Struc-
ture; Balanced Structure   ·   ·   ·   ·   ·   ·   27

CHAPTER III.

THE PARAGRAPH.

Discipline of the Paragraph—(i) Introductory Paragraph—
(ii) Intermediate Paragraph—(iii) Descriptive Paragraph
—(iv) Paragraph of Summary—(v) PREDICATIVE PARA-
GRAPH: Place of Paragraph-Topic; Paragraph-Glide; First
Sentence; General Scheme of Predicative Paragraph;
Copula or Link; The Predicative Matter; A more fully-
developed Scheme of a Predicative Paragraph—MISCEL-
LANEOUS EXAMPLES OF PARAGRAPH-STRUCTURE   ·   ·   87

CHAPTER IV.

FIGURES OF PROSE.

Page

Analogy and Similarity—THE SIMILE: Construction of *Simile*
—THE METAPHOR: Nature of *Metaphor*; Liability to con-
fuse literal words with figurative; Confusion of *Metaphor*;
Length of *Metaphor*; Combination of *Simile* and *Metaphor*;
Personal Metaphor and *Personification*—USE OF FIGURED
PROSE: Figurative Thought; Propriety of Figures; *As
it were*—EPITHETS: Propriety of Epithets; *Synecdoche*;
Metonymy - - - - - - - - - 122

INDEX - - - - - - - - - - 149

ELEMENTS OF PROSE.

CHAPTER I.

ON WRITING IN GENERAL.

ERRATA.

Page 34, line 7. *For* " page 31 " *read* " page 29 ".

,, 54, ,, 6 (from end). *For* " is " *read* " are ".

,, 57, ,, 22. *For* " page 30 " *read* " page 28 ".

,, 57, *footnote*. *For* " page 60 " *read* " page 58 ".

,, 60, line 2. *For* " page 63 " *read* " page 61 ".

., 86, ,, 6. *For* " Anthithesis " *read* " Antithesis ".

· ,, 131, ,, 5 (from end). *For* " page 140 " *read* " page 138 ".

of composition arise in a very large —
the same cause as defects of spelling—a negligent
or lazy habit of mind. In order to write well, it is
first of all necessary to dispossess one's self of the
idea, that, by an intercourse merely casual or desul-

tory even with literature of the best, one may come
by the secret of the craft.

The habit of the student must be eminently the
reflective habit.   He must approach the language
of Shakespeare as he would the language of Molière,
believing that he is no more master of the one
(because it happens to be the language of his daily
use) than he is of the other.   Of the ultimate literary resources of both he is equally ignorant.

A desultory reader, unless he be endowed with
an extraordinarily receptive faculty, will never collect materials for style.   "Out of all that we talk,
or hear others talk through the course of a year,"
says De Quincey, "how much remains on the
memory at the closing day of December?"   "Quite
as little", he adds, "survives from most people's
reading".   A general deposition of matter is no
very sure foundation for exact scholarship; and
the general impressions of the desultory reader
are scarcely more realizable for the formation of
style.

Our native speech is not native to us as a literary
language.   We can never hope fully to realize all
its resources, and must be content to approach it,
on its literary side, as a foreign tongue.   A reflective reader is for ever startled by new manifesta-
tions of its powers: only to the unreflective is there
sameness of utterance; to such a one it never
reveals itself.   It is therefore necessary not merely
to observe, but to meditate upon style.

Yet not all books are to be approached in the
same mind.   I would recommend to the student

two moods for his reading: works of mere information he may absorb in the desultory mood; literature must be approached in the reflective. The language of Shakespeare may not be read in blocks, as it is printed. There are beauties in the prospect that cannot be discovered at a single glance; and, if we miss the beauties themselves, how far are we from discovering the secret of beauty. The growth of every sentence, the sequence of every paragraph, must be watched singly and closely if we are to pluck out the heart of its mystery.

The Necessity of Rules. This reflective habit, then, I would set above all mere rules of rhetoric. Only by such reflective reading may we acquire *taste*—that is, a sense of the right, a perception of the true, in word or phrase, as opposed to the counterfeit. Not that we may ever expect the same precision in grouping our words into meaning, as in grouping our sounds into words. There is no well-defined grouping suited to every thought; nor is it always possible to find the "one apt word" of La Bruyère, language being at best an imperfect and elusive instrument. Nevertheless, in literature of the best, there are to be found words and word-groupings so apt, as almost to be regarded as final. From long and intimate study of these one begins in time to recognize that which rings true in one's own discourse, and to reject that which rings false; the touchstone of truth in words being the perfect adaptation of means to end. Not rules, but reading alone will supply the writer with a word-stock, copious enough to enable him always to select that word which is best adapted to its end.

But the study of writing for the purpose of learning to write is likely to prove far more efficient, if preceded by some knowledge of the accidence of style. Some parts of writing—the structure of the sentence, the correct proportion of the paragraph—are largely mechanical. Familiarity with the mechanism of style makes us the more alert to detect the infinite beauties and varieties of which that mechanism is capable. A knowledge of his accidence supplies the reader with a sure basis of criticism, and renders him the more responsive to the teaching of books.

I would regard, then, some knowledge of the accidence of style as necessary to the intelligent study of literature. But not for this reason alone are rules to be commended. The act of writing is merely one part of composition. The art of rhetoric would be inefficient without the complementary process of criticism. With the beginner in prose it is imperative that first the phrase, then the sentence, then the paragraph, and lastly the whole essay should be submitted to the light of the principles regulating each. The theme, after undergoing such a process, will probably be stiff and self-conscious. "A carefully-written, conscientious, college essay", says Genung, "is stiff and self-conscious. . . . I believe there must be a more or less wooden period in all earnest authorship". But in course of time the rule will become a habit, and at length the habit will grow into an instinct. Then

the written essay will attain the ease and supple-
ness of the spoken word, with the added correctness
that is essential to literary prose.

The Knowledge   It is scarcely necessary to impress
of Words.   upon the beginner in prose the
danger of coining words, or of taking new ways to
his meaning.   It is much more necessary to exhort
him to banish his reasonless fear of words, and to
remember that in diction, sincerity, and sincerity
alone, is power.   By a knowledge of books and
their language he must ensure a ready and copious
supply of words.   Copiousness of vocabulary will
enable him to exercise the power of selection in
regard to those words which, he believes, sincerely
express his meaning.   "A good memory for words",
said the late Prof. Minto, "is no less indispensable
to the author than a good memory for forms is to
the painter".   Be therefore, with De Quincey, "ever
on the watch for a good word".

It is reflective reading that accumulates for the
writer a vocabulary, gives him a sense of the full
power of words, and enables him to adopt such a
placement of them, as will direct the mind of the
reader to the particular meaning he wishes them
to bear.   For it must be remembered that it is not
merely a question of the words we use, but of the
way we use them.   This is very subtly demon-
strated in Russell Lowell's appreciation of the
greatness of Shakespeare:

   " We believe that Shakespeare, like all other great poets,
instinctively used the dialect which he found current, and that
his words are not more wrested from their ordinary meaning

than followed necessarily from the unwonted weight of thought or stress of passion they were called on to support. He needed not to mask familiar thoughts in the weeds of unfamiliar phraseology; for the life that was in his mind could transfuse the language of everyday with an intelligent vivacity that makes it seem lambent with fiery purpose, and at each new reading a new creation. He could say with Dante, that 'no word had ever forced him to say what he would not, though he had forced many a word to say what *it* would not'—but only in the sense that the mighty magic of his imagination had conjured out of it its uttermost secret of power or pathos" (*Shakespeare Once More*, J. R. LOWELL).

There is an insistence on the same point a little later in the essay:

"The secret of force in writing lies not so much in the pedigree of nouns and adjectives and verbs, as in having something that you believe in to say, and making the parts of speech vividly conscious of it".

Not in the dictionary, but only in books, will words reveal to us the secret of their power. Many eminent men have been voracious readers of dictionaries; but we may be tolerably sure that it was not the word but the phrase that they studied. In regard to their own, equally with a foreign language, students should employ the dictionary as a book of quotations, and never relinquish the study of a word until they have acquired the passages in which that word occurs, leaving the recorded dictionary meanings to take care of themselves. Thus the word becomes a living agent to them, not a dry, definable thing.

Insincerity. It is a matter of experience that the beginner in prose sets his heart too much upon display. He longs for the ornate and copious in style; so that "a man" with him may not merely "excel", but must "raise himself to a standard of excellence". It is not sufficient that one be "compelled", but "compelled by force", although the phrase "by force" is wholly inoperative, unless some special "force", as "force of argument", be in question. I have found, indeed, "a more poverty-stricken individual", where the context demanded merely "a poorer man"; and, a still more absurd periphrasis, "when he was in his youthful days", for "in his youth". Desire for the ornate produces an aptness to be pleased with the look rather than with the meaning of a passage; while desire for the copious results in pleonasm and tautology.

This extreme sensibility to the pleasure of look and sound is perhaps the more dangerous habit of the two. It is a species of insincerity, which, in the theme of the beginner, usually takes the form of employing words — periphrases, epithets, and the like—which suggest ideas not consonant with the plainness of the thought, and which break the simple harmonies of prose with a false note of poetry. What we borrow from the prose or poetry of others should be in the nature of treasure-trove; it should be property legally acquired, and at first hand. The gains of Charles Lamb were just gains, yielded by the old folios that he lived and laboured amongst. Ben Jonson, too, says Dryden, "invaded authors like a monarch, and what would be theft in other poets is only victory in him". Very different is the case of the writer who cannot refer to the "pulpit" but as the "sacred

desk ", and is content to avail himself of the thousand chips of poetical expression, worn thin by the
rough usage of time, and strewn on the common
highway of literature.

Though, therefore, the expressions we use are
not inappropriate, they may yet be deficient in
another regard: we may have no sense of property
in them; that is to say, the meaning of the words
may never have been thoroughly acquired, the propriety of the figures may never have been personally investigated. This is a similar fault to that
often found in the themes of students, who, from
laziness or indifference, have caught the diction
of their text-books, without arriving at the sense.
The tone of an author is sooner acquired than his
meaning: a word or phrase is the more readily
remembered, if it be strange to the reader; who frequently uses it again, without being conscious that
the speciality of its force has not been apprehended.
A word has many facets; and if it be strange,
honesty requires that it should not be employed
until it has been viewed from every possible side.
It is our duty to view words, as we view facts, in
the round; and not to rest until we have a total
impression of them.

To reject the meaningless word (meaningless to
the writer, of course, for no word is objectively
meaningless), the tinsel that does but glare, the
epithet that (in its context) signifies nothing—this
is an effort not of the critical, so much as of the
moral faculty. Our desire should be " to see a thing
truly, and to state it just as it is seen and felt ".

If we have at heart the matter of our discourse and the sincere exposition of it, then the matter will so completely dominate the style that all glitter and false show will be shamed away.

The words or phrases we employ may be inoperative, and therefore redundant, from two causes: either because they repeat the sense, or because they add nothing to it. *Tautology* is the name of the one vice; *Pleonasm* of the other. "Neighbouring vicinity" is tautological, because "neighbouring" is an idle anticipation of the meaning of "vicinity"; "compel by force" is pleonastic, because "by force" is no addition to the meaning of "compel".

Tautology. A common form of *Tautology* is a cumulation of synonyms. Our old writers, feeling instinctively the inadequacy of words to convey their meaning (for words *are* inadequate, and the more subtle our meaning is, the harder becomes our struggle for utterance), indulged great licence in regard to synonyms. Than Sir Francis Bacon, "no man", says Ben Jonson, "ever spake more neatly, more presly, more weightily, or suffered less emptiness, less idleness in what he uttered. . . . His hearers could not cough, or look aside from him, without loss". Yet Bacon's prose is crowded with synonyms. In view of Jonson's appreciation, it is instructive to examine when, if ever, these synonyms are "idle". Observe the following passages:

"had his thoughts highly raised by *hopes and expectations* for a time".

"making offer that all things should be guided by her *will and direction*, as the sovereign *patroness and protectress* of the enterprise."

" made it her *design and enterprise*."
" at whose overthrow all her actions should *aim and shoot*."
" and made his *prayers and vows* for *help and deliverance*."
" which *charge and accusation*."

A careful study of these, and other such passages, throws the highest light upon the proper use of synonyms. The second word is idle, only when it repeats the impression created by the first. " Hope" is not " expectation", although it is so often used in that sense, as to render the following word of little meaning; but " will" is certainly not " direction", nor is a " patroness" always a " protectress"; " design" is not " enterprise", " to aim" is not " to shoot". In none of these phrases, therefore, is there *emptiness or idleness* of speech. The same may be said of " prayers and vows" and of " help and deliverance": these expressions tend to diffuseness, but not to vanity; and, if the synonym is employed sincerely, if it is essential or even intentional that the impression should be heightened, the use of the synonym is just. " Charge and accusation" alone is really idle, because it swells the phrase, but not the meaning.

For the same reason, that they *swell the phrase but not the meaning*, the synonyms in the following passages—all characteristic examples taken from students' essays—are tautological:

" whatever may be the nature of his environment, *or of the society in which he mingles*".

" in congenial surroundings, *where he feels in his element*."

" a curious *and uncommon* character."

The italicized parts should, of course, be omitted; they add nothing to the thought.

"too much distressed to take the proper care *they ought* of their dress."	Either "the care they ought" or "the proper care"; not "the proper care they ought".

Words cannot be passive: they must either mend or mar the sense; *obstat quicquid non adjuvat.* Not only, therefore, should we begin with the design of restricting our vocabulary, but we should never hesitate to prune the sentence of superfluously harmful words, even after it is full grown. That "charge *and accusation*" of Bacon's is in the same category with "pride *and arrogance*", "growth *and development*", "universal love *of all*", "confined to him *alone*", "some disputed points *on which critics are not agreed*"; or that still more heinous example quoted by Dr. Blair from an essay of Lord Shaftesbury's: "to mangle *or wound* his outward form *or constitution, his natural limbs or body*". Between such phrases and the following there is a vivid contrast, because in these there is a real accretion to the sense:

"being half-aware of their own dulness, which they call '*common sense*' and '*sound discretion*'".
"In Carlyle's histories the absorbing interest *of succession, of gradual development* is not wanting."

This verbal tautology seems to be indulged on the assumption, that every increase of sound increases the weight of the thought. "It is not uncommon", says Archbishop Whately, "to hear a speaker or writer of this class mentioned as having a 'very fine command of language', when perhaps it might be said with more correctness that 'his language has a command of him'".

Not less pernicious is a certain tautology of thought, frequently to be observed in the work of the beginner in prose. It is illustrated in such a sentence as the following, extracted at random from a student's essay:

"There are institutions, the uses of which do not eloquently appeal to the minds of a large proportion of the community. This, I venture to think, cannot be affirmed of our art galleries, *the invaluable uses of such places being obvious to all.*"

Phrase after phrase, sentence after sentence, in many a student's theme is but an inessential qualification of his meaning. It would appear as if thought were with every one more or less spasmodic; and that, in the intervals, the mind, not having energy enough for invention, gives itself to repetition. It is very common to find an essay, by the deletion of these intervening phrases or sentences, gain not only in power but in consequence; the parts deleted being due to sheer mental idleness or relapse.

These parts, too, are frequently an undue limitation of the writer's meaning:

[The subject was the importance of a home-environment.] "Its moral tone, the habits fostered in it *with regard to cleanliness, tidiness, and order*, the examples set by others, the kindness exercised—all have their influence upon the forming of the individual."

The meaning of "habits" is absurdly limited by the phrase, "with regard to cleanliness, tidiness, and order."

"Now the works of any known author have a practically unlimited sphere of circulation. *Now America and our colonies absorb vast numbers of our books.*"

In each of these examples the second sentence serves as an anti-climax, and as such appreciably weakens the thought.

> "The death of Mr. Gladstone removes one of the most illustrious figures that have adorned the present century. *He has played a very important part in history during the queen's reign.*"

It is consoling to discover Archbishop Whately taxing with this tautologic fault even the writing of Dr. Johnson: "Sentences which might have been expressed as simple ones are expanded into complex ones by the addition of clauses which add little or nothing to the sense, and which have been compared to the false handles and key-holes with which furniture is decorated, that serve no other purpose than to *correspond to the real ones.* Much of Dr. Johnson's writing is chargeable with this fault."

Just as every unnecessary addition to the perfected sentence enfeebles the structure (v. cap. II. p. 30), so every inessential phrase weakens the thought. A writer often blurs the impression he intends to convey in his endeavour to make it more clear. He adds qualifying or explanatory clauses, long after a striking image has been presented to the reader. Observe in the following passage of De Quincey's how the inessential second clause mars the beauty of the first:

> "His station was with the lilies of the field, which toil not neither do they spin: he should have thrown himself upon the admiring sympathies of the world as the most dazzling of rhetorical artists, rather than have challenged their angry passions in a vulgar scuffle for power".

To explain an analogy so easy and clear as this of

"the lilies of the field" is disrespectful to the intelligence of the reader.

Pleonasm. A word or phrase is more idle still, when, without even repeating the meaning, it adds nothing to it. This fault is called *Pleonasm*:

"the landmarks of civilisation were extended *to enclose a greater sphere*".	The italicized phrases add no colour to the thought, and are therefore pleonastic. Delete them.
"from time immemorial *up to the present day.*"	
"admits people *to get through.*"	
"I stamped *with my foot* upon the ground."	

A phrase, however, ceases immediately to be pleonastic when it heightens the colour of a passage. Every one will recognize that "heard with their ears" and "clapped with their hands" have often been found rhetorically effective. The pleonasm most to be avoided by the beginner in prose is the *accumulation of adjuncts.* Do not be afraid of a bare style. It is not essential that every noun should be qualified by an adjective, or every verb by some adverbial attribute; the qualification is too often an abatement, not an increase of power.

From this brief review of some of the "vices" of style, it will be evident that the virtues of writing lie very close to its defects. Consequently, in this part of rhetoric, rules have merely the character of admonitions. Upon faults of expression and diction one may write a homily, but not a treatise. Inspiration counts for much more than instruction, because experience must be acquired personally in the student's own reading, if it is to have a real value. The "artist's eye" in writing is the result of as delicate a training, as in painting.

Before I close this chapter of *admonitions* there are still a few points of general preliminary interest to consider.

Exactness in Speech. It is the curse of words to lose touch with the ideas that they have previously served to express. They are employed inexactly, and become general, and therefore vague, in their application. For this reason we cannot write the language that we speak. The look, the voice, the gesture, endow the spoken word with a meaning it could not otherwise bear, with a meaning that the written word in the same context will never bear. It is a great part of the labour of the writer to restore this lost heritage to words, or to reject them as having no virtue left.

Colloquial words are often vulgar, and more often vague. Precepts against vulgarity should be superfluous; vagueness, it is more difficult to detect. To adjectives like *nice, decent, magnificent, terrible,* and *awful,* to nouns like *arrangement, a lot,* and *a deal* we must strive to restore their lost heritage of meaning; we must employ them particularly, or not at all. In order to indicate the care to be exercised in the avoidance of colloquialism, I record a few examples chosen from students' themes:

COLLOQUIAL.	LITERARY.
" gradually he has all the good in his nature *knocked out of him* by . . ."	" gradually his whole nature is *warped* by . . ."

COLLOQUIAL.	LITERARY.
"*a lot* of their beauty."	"*much* of their beauty."
"the ideas of a person are regulated *a lot* by . . ."	"are *largely* regulated by . . ."
"hundreds of *decent persons*."	"*respectable people*."
"*well up* in the habits of different animals."	"*learned*."
"this was a '*magnificent arrangement*."	"*a great boon*."
"He was *extremely touchy*."	"He was *very irritable*."
"*a great deal* more."	"*much* more."

We must also have a scrupulous care to the speciality of meaning in a word. Let us turn again to a characteristic student-theme:

THE INEXACT WORD.	THE EXACT WORD.
"A thorough discontent *stretched through* the land."	"*pervaded* the land."
"The orator is listened to *with submission*."	"is listened to *with respect*."
"They delight the lover of nature, and *open up* serious food for reflection."	"and *provide* serious food for reflection."
"is able to resist their harmful *effects*."	"their harmful *influences*" (it is hopeless to attempt to resist an "effect").
"with a most *distracted* and despairing look."	"*distraught* and despairing look" ("to distract" is merely "to divert the attention from", *e.g.* "he was distracted by this interruption").
"Several successes were *acquired*."	"Several successes were *gained*" (to *acquire* is "to get hold of").
"a *pleasant* environment does not necessarily elevate the character of the individual."	The special word required is *favourable*.
"*fleshy* corruption."	"*fleshly* corruption."

THE INEXACT WORD.	THE EXACT WORD.
"The Wars of the Roses were *based on* the claim advanced by . . ."	"were *caused by* the claim."
"This might be *neutralized* by . . ."	The special word required was *obviated*.
"richer *brethren*."	The special word required was *countrymen*.
"very *innocent* pursuits."	The special' word required was *insipid*.
"The churchyard presents a spectacle of what Time can do with his *decaying* hand."	"with his *destroying* hand."
"He treated his subject in a *masterful* manner."	"in a *masterly* manner."
"His education was *un-methodical*."	"His education was *un-systematic*."

It was on this principle that the old rhetoricians proclaimed the excellence of "proper" terms, that is, words which produce a clear and special image. For an indefinite discourse is invariably ineffective:

"When it came from the furnace it weighed 56 tons, and was 42 inches thick. When it had passed between the rollers to and fro several times, it had lost half its thickness and *a great deal of its weight*."

How chilling to the interest of the reader is that last uncertain phrase, *a great deal of its weight*.

Simplicity. I would not advance mere simplicity as a cardinal quality of style. To write with simplicity is not always necessary, and not always possible. It is the aptness of the word, not its simplicity, that should be the first care. A writing may be perspicuous, of which the diction is abstruse, if the words are apt. Precision, indeed, will often have the effect of rendering a passage

not simple but abstruse to the careless reader; aptness of vocabulary is often opposed to simplicity.
But the duty of the writer ends, when, having
given to his constructions as correct a turn as
possible, he has afforded the reader all the help in
his power. Clearness of structure, not simplicity
of language, is the great thing: without this, as
Blair finely expresses it, " the richest ornaments of
style only glimmer through the dark". In other
words, the perspicuity, and therefore half the pleasure, of prose is largely attainable by mechanical
means. There is no part of style which so well
repays study, or which demands so little native
genius as this. For, while the choice of words is
a matter of taste and experience, the structure of
the sentence is part of the " book-work " of style.

Clearness. "Study clear ideas" is a favourite
canon of prose; and, indeed, idleness
and vanity of writing does most frequently arise
from dark and clouded thinking. A writer who, because his conception is indistinct and formless, has
lost his way in a subject only gets into more difficult places by attempting new ways to his meaning.
He must begin again. On the other hand, the pos-
session of clear ideas does not necessarily involve
clearness of expression. A writer is often apt to be
deceived by his knowledge of his own meaning;
himself perfectly master of what he intends to say,
he may read into his words a sense which they in
fact do not bear. Just as, when listening to an
Handelian chorus, one, having the words of the text
in his memory, may read a sense into music that to

another appears only as successive waves of musical sound. Indistinctness of conception is inevitably a cause of obscurity. But there may be equal obscurity where the conception is distinct; unless the writer encourages in himself the habit of surveying his sentences objectively, that is, from the reader's side.

Harmony. With the ancients, Cicero and Quintilian, harmony was regarded as the highest excellence. They held, justly of course, that prose should have its harmony as well as verse; and wrote copiously on the principles even of quantity in prose. But with them the appeal to the senses was more pronounced than it is with us. Moreover, the liberty of their structure, with its liquidity of inflection, its freedom from form-words and auxiliaries, combined to render their language much more susceptible to harmony than ours. We are fonder of precision than of "tune" in prose.

As a matter of fact, there is nothing more pernicious to the style of the beginner in prose than a persistent striving after harmony. He lives in continual dread of simplicity and abruptness. It is harmony, or what he believes to be such, that deceives him into the use of words which render the phrase more turgid, but do not swell the sense; words which, until they have grown familiar to him in his daily talk or reading, he should not venture to use in composition. For sincerity, the first virtue of all style, depends upon an unerring perception of the various powers of the words we employ. The writer who expresses the simple thought "makes us wish ourselves there" by "induces a desire to be transported to that delightful locality", fails to recognize the unfitness of means to end. The words are pleasing to him apparently because they are strange; he does not perceive their inherent *untruth*. He has yet to learn that the higher vocabulary has uses as exact as the lower. A simple thought requires simplicity of diction. It is only the more subtle shades of thought and feeling that require for their proper discrimination hard words and "inkhorn" terms.

Sense has its harmony as well as sound. That disposition of phrase and clause which secures the most precise impression will at the same time secure the most harmonious. A straggling phrase, like a broken chord, mars the music of a sentence, because it injures the meaning. A well-disposed and compacted period is always harmonious, because it faithfully serves the sense; and in the one apt word which fits the thought, the "other harmony" of prose resides. It is invariably perfect sense that causes perfect sound.

A Last Word. A last word to the beginner in prose. Allow your own personality to shine through the medium you use, by being absolutely true to yourself, not affecting an interest that you do not feel, not employing phrases whose full import you do not comprehend, not attempting to assist a defective imagination by laboured beauties. Bishop Butler considered it a cardinal quality of style to write "with simplicity and in earnest", a precept which was simply interpreted by Archbishop Whately as "speaking as if one has something to say". Assume that the reader has a desire for knowledge, and let your single purpose be to write so that you may be clearly and absolutely understood. Do not in the beginning aim at extrinsic graces, or harmony: let the beauty of your prose be the beauty of sense; the pleasure of your prose, its perfect intelligibility. With this regard, everyone has the making of a writer, whom Nature endows with a language to use.

<hr>

CHAPTER II.

THE SENTENCE.

I. SENTENCE-UNITY.

THE GRAMMATICAL VIEW.

A Single Proposition. In speaking, even though we may introduce impertinent matter into our periods, we may, by stress, pause, and intonation, fix the attention of the hearer upon the principal subject. But, in writing, the most insignificant departure will puzzle and irritate; because modulation, and the whole art of voice-gesture, is suggested but barely by mechanical means. The earliest restraint, therefore, to which the writer must submit, arises from the necessity of preserving in every sentence a singleness of aim; so that it may produce upon the mind of the reader unity of impression.

The writer, within the limits of his period-stops, must never for a moment shift his point of view; where his mind settles at first, there for the time it must rest.

Every written sentence, then, must contain a single proposition with or without particulars, these to be strictly relevant. Particulars may be introduced (1) by means of subordinate clauses; (2) by dividing the whole sentence into co-ordinate parts.

Subordinate Clauses. It is not easy to destroy the single-ness of impression, to be derived from a sentence, by means of Adverb-clauses (Time, Place, Cause, Condition, and so forth); still less dangerous is the Substantive-clause, because this enters even more intimately into the structure, as Subject, Object, or Complement. It is the Adjective-clause that requires real care: the reason for which is that the Adjective-clause is of twofold nature; as illustrated in the following sentence:

"The idol *which*[1] they seem to address strides like a colossus over the door of the inner temple, *which*[2] here as with the Jews is esteemed the most sacred part of the building".

Here *which*[1] introduces a clause that limits or defines the word "idol", chains our idea of "idol" down to the "idol they address"; the clause is therefore of a *restrictive* nature. But *which*[2] does not so limit the phrase "inner temple" as to restrict the mind to some particular "inner temple"; it is really equivalent to "and this": the clause is therefore of a *continuating* nature. To "continue" an idea irrelevantly by means of an adjective-clause is as easy as it is dangerous. In the above sentence, indeed, there is unity of impression; but the following example shows how easily a writer may be allured by an adjective-clause into by-ways of thought:

"The peasants are often of a sullen and revengeful disposition, greatly given to anarchy, *which is the sure sign of prevalent discontent*".

Here, after the natural close of the sentence, comes a straggling clause that is not in the least relative to the thought which precedes. Beware, then, of the adjective-clause as the only really dangerous inducement to digression in a complex sentence.

Co-ordinate Elements. The danger that lurks in the "Continuating Adjective-clause" is ever-present in some types of the compound sentence.

Between the co-ordinate elements of the compound sentence, there may exist *four* possible relations, indicated respectively by the four conjunctions: "and", "but", "or", "therefore".

(i) *Cumulative* ("and"): Sentences are properly cumulative, only when each refers intimately to one and the same central thought or action.

"Here he lived by hunting; and was obliged to supply every day a certain proportion of the spoil to regale his savage masters."

"His looks were pale, thin, and sharp; round his neck he wore a broad black riband; his coat was trimmed with tarnished twist. . . ."

In such sentences as the following, it is quite clear that the parts are not strictly co-ordinate, but that each suggests a different centre of thought:

"The present education of the English people surpasses that of people who lived in former days; and one of the essentials of sound learning is the thorough and careful reading of good books".

(1) Education of English.

(2) Essentials of sound education in general.

"The memory is decidedly a natural gift, although much may be done to improve it; and study will also be necessary to the thorough understanding of a language."

(1) Memory improved by study.

(2) Language also has to be learned by study.

In the above examples it will be observed that the second thought runs tangentially from the circumference, instead of radiating from the centre—a very common fault.

(ii) *Adversative* ("but"): Again, the second proposition must radiate from the same central idea, in order to be properly "opposed" to the first:

"He takes as much pains to hide his feelings as any hypocrite would, to conceal his indifference; but, on every unguarded moment, the mask drops off and reveals him to the most superficial observer".

But observe the following:

"The Dutch are most prosaic; but we must admire their great enterprise in regaining their country from the sea".

A centre of thought is suggested in the word "prosaic"; yet in the same sentence we pass tangentially to speak of "the Dutch", who are on the thought-circumference. There is, consequently, no just antithesis in the thought, and the parts of the sentence are not truly co-ordinate. "Enterprise" and "prosaic nature" are not in "opposition", because they are not related to the same centre of thought. Again:

"A child trained in a good home and surrounded by healthy home-influences generally grows up to honourable manhood; while, on the other hand, a child brought up in an untidy home is untidy and unmethodical when he becomes a man".

Here again the two propositions do not run from the same centre; it is quite preposterous to oppose "honourable manhood" to "untidiness".

(iii) *Alternative* ("or"), *e.g.*:

"The words a man uses may express his idea, but not quite fully and completely; or they may express it together with something more than he intends".

(iv) *Illative* ("for" and "therefore"): Errors of Cause and Effect belong rather to logic than to rhetoric.

Neither the Illative nor the Alternative parts of a sentence are easily made destructive to unity. Real danger lies in (1) the Adjective-clause, (2) the Cumulative Sentence, and (3) the Adversative Sentence. Take care that the thoughts in all sentences be as *radii* from a given centre, and not as *tangents* from the circumference.

THE RHETORICAL VIEW.

Blair's Rules for Sentence-unity. This is the case for Unity in the Sentence, as it appears from a purely grammatical view. A general survey of the whole ground from the rhetorical position will serve but to lay further emphasis upon these grammatical features. As starting-points for this rhetorical survey, we may take the *Rules* laid down by BLAIR in his *Lectures on Rhetoric and Belles Lettres* (Lect. xi.).

(i) "*In the first place, during the course of the sentence, the scene should be changed as little as possible.*"

This, interpreted metaphorically as well as literally, is a precept of wide and useful application. It applies literally, of course, to descriptive sentences. It is here often difficult to establish a central idea; we must decide by nearness of relationship.

"Then he rapped on the *door* with a bit of stick like a handspike that he carried; and, when my father appeared, called roughly for a glass of wine."	The scene has a given centre, though not a central idea—*door*.
"I *walked* along beside the surf with great enjoyment; till, thinking I was now got far enough to the south, I took the cover of some thick bushes, and *crept* warily up to the ridge of the spit."	The actions are very nearly related, and referred to a central action —*walked*.
"He, for his part, took a great draught of the wine, and spoke with the most unusual solemnity."	

Frequently, however, even in a descriptive sentence, it is quite possible to fix a definite *centre of thought*, in which case, of course, the danger of "changing the scene" disappears.

"By his own *account* he must have lived his life among some of the wickedest men that God ever allowed upon the sea; and the language in which he told these *stories* shocked our plain country-people almost as much as the crimes that he described."	Both parts of the sentence have a common centre, referred to in the words *account* and *stories*.
"Every man on board seemed well *content*, and they must have been hard to please if they had been otherwise; for it is my belief that there was never a ship's crew so spoiled since Noah put to sea.'	Common centre: *content*.

"At first I had *supposed* 'the dead man's chest' to be that identical big box of his upstairs in the front room; and the *thought* had been mingled in my nightmares with that of the one-legged seafaring man."

Common centre, referred to in the words *supposed* and *thought.*

"It was Silver's *voice*, and, before I had heard a dozen *words*, I would not have shown myself for all the world, but lay there trembling and *listening* in the extreme of fear and curiosity; for, from these dozen *words*, I understood that the lives of all the honest men aboard depended upon me alone."

Common centre: *words.*

When the scene is actually changed, a common centre may often be established by a careful disposition of the sentence. In the example Blair gives:

"After we came to anchor they put me on shore, where I was welcomed by all my friends, who received me with the greatest kindness",

unity of impression is lost, not because the ideas have no connection with one another, but because, as Blair says, "by shifting so often both the place and the person, *we* and *they* and *I* and *who*, they appear in such a disunited view that the sense of connection is almost lost". By skilful subordination, unity of impression may be restored, thus:

"Having come to an anchor, *I was put on shore*, where I was welcomed by all my friends, and received with the greatest kindness."

There is now a common centre for the sentence: *I was put on shore.*

(ii) "*Never to crowd into one sentence things which have so little connection that they could bear to be divided into two or three sentences.*"

It has already been remarked that this rule may be transgressed (1) by threading in an adjective-clause, and (2) by cumulating sentences that have in fact no co-ordinate bond between them. The examples given by Blair may be examined in connection with the instance of a fatal adjective-clause given above (page 31).

"In this uneasy state, both of his public and private life, Cicero was oppressed by a new and cruel affliction, the death of his daughter Tullia; which happened soon after her divorce from Dolabella, *whose manners and humours were entirely disagreeable to her.*"

"Archbishop Tillotson died in this year. He was exceedingly beloved both by King William and Queen Mary, *who nominated Dr. Tennison, Bishop of Lincoln, to succeed him.*"

This general precept, however, may be levelled against all kinds of heterogeneous sentences:

"In the north the Marquis of Newcastle secured all the country, garrisoned York, Scarborough, Carlisle, Newcastle, Pomfret, Leeds, and all the considerable places, and took the field with a very good army,[1] though afterwards he proved more unsuccessful than the rest, having the whole power of a kingdom at his back, the Scots coming in with an army to the assistance of the parliament;[2] which indeed was the general turn of the scale of the war; for, had it not been for the Scots army, the king had most certainly reduced the parliament, at least to good terms of peace, in two years' time."[3]

First, by stating as a concessive clause (*though*) what is really not a subordinate statement; and then, by adjoining a straggling adjectival clause (*which*) the author glides into two separate digressions. There are consequently *three* sentences instead of one. Reconstruct as follows:

"(1) In the north . . . a very good army. (2) Afterwards, however, he proved . . . parliament. (3) This, indeed, was . . . two years' time."

"The king was the third article: his force at Shrewsbury I have noted already; the alacrity of the

In this sentence, and in the following, a common centre may be established, and unity

gentry filled him with hopes, and all his army with vigour, *and the 8th of October, 1642, his majesty gave orders to march.*"

"The enemy lost about 3000 men, and we carried near 150 prisoners, with 500 horses, some standards and arms, and, among the prisoners, their colonel, *but he died, a little after, of his wounds.*"

of impression restored by sub-ordination, e.g.:

". . . the alacrity of the gentry filled him with such hopes, and all his army with such vigour, that on the 8th of October, 1642, his majesty gave orders to march."

Write:

". . . and, among the prisoners, their colonel, *who, however, died a little after of his wounds*". The fact of the colonel's death, if properly subordinated, is really in unity with the rest of the sentence, because by death he was removed from the number of the prisoners."

(iii) "*To keep clear of all parentheses in the middle of them.*"

This is a matter of discretion. Let us say rather:

See that the parentheses radiate from the same thought-centre. A high degree of picturesqueness is often attained by bracketing one sentence within another.

"This is the question (and a very nice and subtle one it is) which we are now to discuss."

"The honest hands—and I was soon to see it proved that there were such on board—must have been very stupid fellows."

(iv) "*To bring it always to a full and perfect close.*"

"I need not take notice", says Blair, "that an unfinished sentence is no sentence at all according to any grammatical rule. But very often we meet with sentences that are, so to speak, more than finished." All that impairs the unity of a sentence (straggling adjective-clauses, falsely co-ordinated elements, &c.) destroys also its natural climax. But it should also be noticed that, by leaving some insignificant word, phrase, or clause to hang like a loose thread at the end of the fabric, while we do not affect the unity, we may yet mar the climax of the sentence. Adverbs, adverb-clauses, conjunctions, and prepositions should, if possible, be packed into the body of the period.

IMPERFECT CLIMAX.	"THE FULL AND PERFECT CLOSE."
"in such a manner as to prevent ambiguity *altogether*."	"in such a manner as *altogether* to prevent ambiguity."
"From these shall emanate all that is necessary to fit the individual to play his part in life, *as far as education is concerned*."	"From these shall emanate all that is necessary, *as far as education is concerned*, to fit the individual to play his part in life."
"Since it appears impossible to delight, I shall endeavour to instruct *merely*."	". . . I shall endeavour *merely* to instruct."
"The oddities that marked his character began to appear *soon*."	"*soon* began to appear", or "began *soon* to appear".
"This was the end that his whole policy aimed *at*."	"This was the end *at* which his whole policy aimed."
"My curiosity began to abate *by this time*."	"My curiosity began *by this time* to abate."
"The cat escaped, *however*."	"The cat, *however*, escaped."
"This is a habit that I always indulge *in*."	"This is a habit *in* which I always indulge."

II. SENTENCE-STRUCTURE.

GRAMMATICAL STRUCTURE.

Modern English being a language almost devoid of inflection, the exact function of a word or phrase is frequently to be determined only by its context.

The parts of an English Sentence are, therefore, grammatically subject to *a fixed order*:

(i) The Subject should precede; and the Object, Predicate-noun, &c., should follow the Predicate.

(ii) Words or phrases intimately related must be juxtaposed (*Law of Proximity*).

(iii) Adjuncts, attributive and qualifying, should precede their head-words (*Law of Priority*).

It is, however, necessary to remember that—

(1) This grammatical order is quite conventional, being by no means identical with the psychological order; *e.g.* "Will you pass the mustard?" occurs to the mind as (1) mustard, (2) pass, (3) you. The grammatical order of words is therefore frequently in conflict with the order of thought.

(2) All parts of the sentence are not equal in stress-value: the Beginning and the End are positions of far greater emphasis than the Middle.

(3) There is no readier method of giving prominence to a word or phrase than by departing from the grammatical order.

Consequently, even in an English sentence, where the precise office of the word depends so much upon its position, there is considerable liberty allowed for rhetorical effect; our general purpose being to throw really significant words and phrases into bold relief, and to divert the reader's attention from those that are not so highly essential to the meaning. At the same time we must remember that the natural strength of the *rhetorical order* arises from the fact that it is abnormal; if, therefore, we depart from the *grammatical order* too freely, or without

adequate provocation, we impair the effectiveness
of the perversion.

THE ADVERB AND ADVERB-PHRASE.

Before we proceed to consider how far and with
what objects we may venture to pervert this fixed
grammatical order, it will be well to examine the
disposition of the one class of words, whose order
in an English sentence is still comparatively free—
the *adverb*, *adverb-phrase*, and *adverb clause*.

There is nothing more difficult than skilfully to
pack the sentence with the necessary adverbial
adjuncts. "It ought to be always held a rule",
says Blair, "not to crowd such circumstances together, but rather to intermix them with more
capital words in such different parts of the sentence
as can admit them naturally."

There are *three* leading principles which guide
the "intermixing" of adverbial terms.

Rule I.—Jux-
taposition.   THEY MUST BE PLACED AS NEAR AS
POSSIBLE TO THEIR "CAPITAL WORDS".

In illustration of the importance of this law of
proximity in its application to adverbs and adverb-
phrases, observe the following constructions:

PLACEMENT FAULTY.	PLACEMENT CORRECT.
(Consequently the meaning is fre-quently ambiguous, and the end of the sentence is often weak.)	
"The chapter on the state of society in 1685 has been con-victed of many exaggerated statements by less dazzling antiquarians."	The chapter on the state of society in 1685 has been, by less dazzling antiquarians, convicted of many exaggerated statements.
"He could observe his own faults in others clearly enough."	He could observe clearly enough his own faults in others.

PLACEMENT FAULTY	PLACEMENT CORRECT.
"The voice repeated the demand again."	The voice again repeated the demand.
"This may in great part be authentic."	This may be in great part authentic.
"I am now completely restored to health after having been at death's door through having taken five bottles of your medicine."	After having been at death's door, I am now completely restored to health through having taken five bottles of your medicine.
The annual meeting will be held at the Council House on Tuesday next of a very deserving philanthropic enterprise.	On Tuesday next, will be held at the Council House the annual meeting of a very deserving philanthropic enterprise.

In speaking, stress and modulation frequently serve to determine the reference of the adverb; but in writing, such a loose construction as,

"I merely came to inform you of the fact",

to express the idea.

"I came merely to inform you of the fact",

is quite inadmissible.

In this example, and in some of the others given above, it will be noticed, not only that the modifying word or words should be *juxtaposed* to their head-words, but that, especially in the case of simple adverbs, they should generally *precede* their head-words.

Order of Adverb and Verb. A simple adverb, indeed, invariably precedes an adjective or another adverb (exception: *enough, e.g.* "strong enough for anything"). When it modifies a verb or verbal, its order is subject to the following rules:

(1) A simple adverb should lie between the auxiliary and the participle (or infinitive), if it modify the latter;

(2) but before the auxiliary, if it modify the whole predicate.

(3) It may either precede or follow the simple verb or verbal.

Examples:

(1) We should never appear angry. I was lately invited to a visitation dinner. Each had pretty well satisfied his own appetite.	Adverb modifies participle or infinitive.
(2) You will probably be pleased to see my letter dated from Terki.	Adverb modifies whole predicate.
(3) They now found time to press others. He greatly rejoiced at their misfortune (or "rejoiced greatly"). Gently to reprove is better than chastisement (or, "to reprove gently").	Adverb modifying a simple verb or verbal.

It would seem from Rule 3 that the order of an adverb modifying a simple verb or verbal is quite indifferent. This, however, is not actually the case. There is a difference in meaning and stress-value. The natural order of the adverb is *after* the simple verb; there it has full stress-value and also full meaning. In literary prose it is very liable to front order, because there it has less stress-value and frequently less meaning.

Contrast:

ADVERB EMPHATIC. (Retains always its full meaning.)	ADVERB UNEMPHATIC. (Frequently loses some of its meaning.)
He came suddenly into the town.	He suddenly came into the town.
I told him quietly all he desired to know.	I quietly told him all he desired to know.
I mastered it thoroughly.	I thoroughly mastered it.
I ran quickly to his assistance.	I quickly ran to his assistance.

ADVERB EMPHATIC.	ADVERB UNEMPHATIC.
He told me then that I was wrong.	He then told me that I was wrong.
I propose now to speak to the second indictment.	I now propose to speak to the second indictment.
This remains still a mystery (or "a mystery still").	This still remains a mystery.
Following quickly in his footsteps.	Quickly following in his footsteps.
He slept often during the day.	He often slept during the day.
To consider fully this point.[1]	Fully to consider this point.

"Only", "merely", "not", &c. There are, however, some simple adverbs to which change of order can give neither additional stress-value nor increased significance, *e.g. only, merely, even, not.* These are merely qualifying words; consequently their relation to their head-word is peculiarly intimate. To prevent ambiguity, they should always *immediately precede* the very words to which they refer.

"He was not even pleased when I told him he had succeeded"

is different in meaning from:

"He was not pleased, even when I told him he had succeeded."

Distinguish also:

"He was not required to do it"

from

"He was required not to do it."

By

"I am only going to take one part of it"

[1] In regard to the order of adverb and verbal, the student should further remark that, while literary prose admits indifferently the positions:

to reprove gently,	gently to reprove,
to consider fully,	fully to consider,

the "split infinitive" order ("to gently reprove", "to fully consider") belongs exclusively to colloquial usage. This unsightly break, unknown to the older language, and even to early modern English, is still unknown in correct prose; although the exigences of verse admit it.

is invariably intended

"I am going to take only one part of it",

and should therefore be so disposed. In the same way,

"We only succeed when we begin to exert ourselves"

should of course be

"We succeed only when we begin to exert ourselves".

Correlative Adverbs   This invariable principle applies also to *adverbial couples*: "not $\begin{cases} \text{only} \\ \text{merely} \end{cases}$ . . . but", "so much . . . as", "partly . . . partly", "not . . . but", "either . . . or", "neither . . . nor", "rather . . . than", &c. Such correlative adverbs serve to balance the ideas of the sentence; and this balance is quite impaired by careless placement. Contrast the effect of correct and faulty placement in the following sentences:

PLACEMENT FAULTY.	PLACEMENT CORRECT.
I not only mean that he is wrong, but that he is conscious of being wrong.	I mean not only that he is wrong, but that he is conscious of being wrong.
It is not merely necessary to observe, but to meditate.	It is necessary not merely to observe, but to meditate.
This is not so much due to generosity, as to a sense of justice.	This is due not so much to generosity, as to a sense of justice.
This is partly derived from one source, partly from another.	This is derived partly from one source, partly from another.
He did not intend to injure, but only to deceive us.	He intended not to injure, but only to deceive us.
The real danger did not lie without, but within the state.	The real danger lay not without, but within the state.
They are deceived either by similarity of sound or sense.	They are deceived by similarity either of sound or sense.
I was neither impressed by the expediency nor the prudence of such an act.	I was impressed neither by the expediency nor the prudence of such an act.
I was rather impressed by his manner than his matter.	I was impressed rather by his manner than his matter.

Rule II.—Relative Value of Adverbs. *Cæteris paribus,* ADVERB-PHRASES SHOULD OCCUR IN THE FOLLOWING ORDER: (*a*) TIME, (*b*) PLACE, (*c*) OTHER ABSTRACT RELATIONS, SUCH AS MANNER, CAUSE, QUANTITY, &C.

PLACEMENT FAULTY.	PLACEMENT CORRECT.
She had stayed out with the Countess at the Gardens all night.	She had stayed out all night at the Gardens with the Countess.

This order may be subject to perversion under the following conditions:

(1) A simple adverb may precede an adverb-phrase:

A year afterwards he came suddenly into the town,

where the single adverb of manner takes order before the adverb-phrase of place.

(2) End-position may be given to an emphatic adverb or adverb-phrase:

She had stayed out at the Gardens with the Countess all night.

Further perversion of the order may be required by RULE III.

Rule III.—Adverb Phrase in Front-position. IF THE ADVERB-PHRASE BE COMPARATIVELY HEAVY, OR IF IT QUALIFY THE WHOLE IDEA OF THE SENTENCE, IT SHOULD TAKE FRONT-POSITION IN THE SENTENCE.

PLACEMENT FAULTY.	PLACEMENT CORRECT.
My curiosity began to abate by this time.	By this time my curiosity began to abate, *or*, began by this time to abate.
I went to meet him at the gate of the garden on the eleventh hour, pursuant to his information.	Pursuant to his information, I went on the eleventh hour to meet him at the gate of the garden.

PLACEMENT FAULTY.	PLACEMENT CORRECT.
They continued the debate with equal acerbity on both sides, for eleven hours on the same day, without arriving at a definite policy.	For eleven hours on the same day, with equal acerbity on both sides they continued the debate, without arriving at a definite policy.
We ought to place ourselves in his position, in order properly to judge his action.	In order properly to judge his action, we ought to place ourselves in his position.
The whole party sat down as soon as they had gained the brow of the ascent, partly from the damping influence of this alarm, partly to rest Silver and the sick folk.	Partly from the damping influence of this alarm, partly to rest Silver and the sick folk, the whole party sat down as soon as they had gained the brow of the ascent.

In regard to RULE III., it should be remarked:

(1) Apart from the adverb-phrase that is removed to the front of the sentence, the rest should follow, as far as possible, the order prescribed by RULE II.

Pursuant to his information, I went on the eleventh hour [*Time*] to meet him at the gate of the garden [*Place*].

(2) Although in the case of the simple adverb (since its usual position is *after* the verb, and in any case it is packed into the body of the sentence), front-position is emphatic:

"Home he returns, with a full cry against the Church of England";

yet an adverb-phrase in a front position has a very small stress-value; its *qualification* also is of so general a kind, that it is really of minor significance to its own sentence: we do not linger on it, expecting its presence to be justified by what succeeds, as is the case with the simple adverb or the adverb-clause holding this prominent position.

(3) In fact, its presence is justified rather by what precedes; for it is more clearly related to the previous sentence than to its own. Consequently, it is a *connective* (or *sentence-glide*) of the most effective kind:

" *With this design*, I lately went to see the entry of a foreign ambassador ".	Sentence-glide.
" *In the same manner*, a crowd gather round a dog suspected of madness."	ditto.

It should be noticed that the very insignificance of these fronted adverb-phrases, combined with their prominent position, naturally attracts the attention to what precedes; that, in some cases, they obviously repeat the leading idea of the previous sentence, and, were it not for their connective function, would be quite tautological.

THE ADVERB CLAUSE.

Front-order. It has been seen that, when the adverb-phrase "sweepingly qualifies" the principal statement, it should come first; partly because in such a case a knowledge of the attendant circumstance is necessary to the full appreciation of this principal statement. On much stronger ground, when the *Adverb-clause* introduces an attendant circumstance that is vital to the meaning of the principal sentence, this clause should precede. It is difficult to lay down any precise rule in this regard but it may be remarked that, in general, Clauses of

    (i) Time ('when', 'while', 'before' 'after', &c.),
    (ii) Condition ('if'),
    (iii) Concession ('though'),

(iv) Reason (when introduced by 'as', 'since'), are vital to the meaning of the principal sentence, and should consequently *precede* it. Thus in the following sentences, suspension in structure will in general be found necessary to prevent suspension of the meaning; if we are *at once* to see the sentence 'whole' (which is one of the chief aims of rhetoric), we must delay the principal statement:

"In eating, *after nature is once satisfied*, every additional morsel brings stupidity and distemper with it".

"*When we were got in*, he welcomed us to his house with great ceremony."

"*If I should run hunting after all these fine folk*, what should I get for my journey but an appetite?"

"*Though there happens to be no likeness*, a Countess offered me an hundred for its fellow."

"*As there were several others flying in the same manner*, we passed without notice."

Of these four kinds of clause, however, the Clause of Time is often not vital to the meaning, and may consequently follow·

"He paused, *when he had got into a sitting position on the edge*".

Frequently suspension is impossible with a Clause of Time; for 'when', 'till', &c., may be co-ordinate (cumulative) in value (= and then).

"We rode hard all the way, *till we drew up before Dr. Livesey's door.*"

"I fancied myself, as it were, awakened out of a dream; *when* (= and then) *I saw this region of prodigies restored to woods and rivers, fields and meadows.*"

End-Order. Clauses of
    (v) Consequence ('that'),
 (vi) Comparison ('than'),
 (vii) Reason (introduced by 'because'),

should *succeed.*

The very nature of 'that' (consequence) and 'than' clauses demands that they should follow the principal sentence.

> "I tore my shoe in such a manner *that I was utterly un-qualified to march forward with the main body.*"
> "Surer to prosper *than prosperity could have assured us.*"

The 'than' clause (which is usually elliptical) may, however, precede (*a*) for emphasis, (*b*) for continuity.

> (*a*) Than this, there is no stronger plea.
> (*b*) "which, when Beelzebub perceived—than whom, Satan except, none higher sat."
> "as seek to soften that (than which what's harder?), his Jewish heart."

The 'Reason' clause should not follow, unless it is co-ordinate in value; conversely whenever the Clause of Reason does follow, it is better to use the co-ordinating conjunction 'because'.

> "The great folks you saw pass by just now have five hundred friends, *because they have no occasion for them.*"

The 'as', 'since', are *misused* in the following:

> "She hoped to be excused, *as* she had stayed out all night at the Gardens with the Countess".
> "yet it is very surprising too, *as* I had her from a Parliament man, a friend of mine in the Highlands."
> "A debauch of wine is even more pardonable than this, *since* one glass insensibly leads on to another."

Free-Order.

The Clause of

(viii) Purpose ('that')

hangs very free in the sentence. It is placed as emphasis or continuity may require; front-position being most emphatic.

"I always love to keep my prospects at home, *that my friends may come to see me the oftener.*"

"I will be assured I may; and, *that I may be assured,* I will bethink me." (Balance, Continuity, Emphasis, demand that the clause of purpose should here precede.)

RHETORICAL STRUCTURE.

INVERSION.

Reasons of Inversion. The possibilities of *Inversion* in English prose are many; the opportunities comparatively few. There are two valid excuses for Inversion: (1) Emphasis, (2) Continuity. The more valid of the two is Continuity, because the most sequential sentence is invariably the most emphatic.

The two following inversions are purely emphatic:

"A chapter upon German rhetoric would be in the same ludicrous predicament as Van Troil's chapter on the snakes of Iceland, which delivers its business in one summary sentence, announcing that—*snakes in Iceland there are none.*"	A very broken order.
"But next upon the roll comes forward an absolute charlatan; a charlatan, *the most accomplished* that can ever have figured upon so intellectual a stage."	Adjective after Noun—unusual save where there are three or four adjectives attributive to the same noun.

The following inversion, however, is to secure continuity:

INSEQUENTIAL AND WEAK.	SEQUENTIAL AND STRONG.
Richard's faults are all forgotten in the pity excited by his miserable fall; and Shakespeare has taken care to intensify *this feeling*.	Richard's faults are all forgotten in the pity excited by his miserable fall; and *this feeling* Shakespeare has taken care to intensify.

Generally, by means of various adverbs, adverb-phrases, adverb-clauses, or by purely connective terms, we are enabled to glide easily, without change of order, from one sentence to the next; *e.g.*:

" But, *though the nation be exempt from real evils*, think not, my friend, that it is on this account more happy than others ".	Adverb - clause, recapitulatory and purely connective.

But when continuity is not to be attained by this means, to ensure a natural *sentence-glide*, Inversion must be employed.

The chief Inversions it is possible to effect in modern English are the following:

Inversion of Subject and Predicate. (1) *Inversion of Subject and Predicate.*—This is commonly effected in prose by means of a leading adverb or adverb-phrase.

An adverb, according to the Law of Proximity, always exerts a power of attraction[1] over the verb.

---

[1] This attraction is peculiarly powerful, when the preceding adverb or adverb-phrase has a negative value; *e.g.*:

> *Never was* there a greater catastrophe.
> *Not till to-morrow will* I relate it.
> *Not often do* we find.
> *Scarcely had* he spoken.
> *Not only does* he preach.

Consequently, when an adverb stands at the head of the sentence, inversion is common. The conditions favourable to inversion are (*a*) a *light* verb, and (*b*) a *heavy* subject.

(*a*) *a light verb.* Contrast:

THE VERB LIGHT.	THE VERB HEAVY.
	Inversion is inadvisable.
There died King Henry.	There King Henry was killed.
Then came George.	Then George succeeded.

If, however, the verb is encumbered, by a second modifier, even though it be *light* of itself, inversion is very unusual. Contrast:

Then came George.	Then George came to the throne.

(*b*) *a heavy subject.*

The lightest subject, and consequently the subject least capable of receiving emphasis by inversion, is the pronoun *I*; only when the verb is quite insignificant, as in *said I*, may inversion take place. Contrast:

Now I came.	Now came he.

A noun, being a notional word, is a subject of more weight than a pronoun, which is a purely relational word. Contrast:

He cried.	Cried the king.

Thus we see that the heavier the subject, the greater the liability to inversion. Inversion, without the attraction of a leading adverb, is not possible in prose, except where the verb is very insignificant, *e.g. cried, said.* But with a leading adverb, and a heavy subject, inversion is very common. It imparts:

(i) **a proper dignity to the subject.**

"Then comes an affecting history of a little boy bit in the leg by a mad dog."

"Down that broad shaded lane stands the house of the squire."

(ii) **a harmony to the sentence, by balancing to-gether the really significant parts.**

"There fluttered a sheet of manuscript; there, a torn handkerchief."

(iii) **a continuity to the sentence, by ensuring a just connection between related parts.**

STRUCTURE FAULTY.	STRUCTURE CORRECT.
"*The sun gleamed* dimly through the fog, which now gave little more light than the moon."	Dimly through the fog *gleamed the sun*, which now gave little more light than the moon.

Inversion of Predicative Word. (2) *Displacement of Predicate-adjective or Predicate-noun.*—This may be desirable

(i) for emphasis, and
(ii) for continuity (or connection).

"*Very fine* they are, master."	Sentence-glide.
"*A great orator* he was not, but *an excellent debater* he certainly was."	Two balanced phrases in a prominent position.
"The damage is infinite knowledge receives by it."	The want of connection renders the sentence ambiguous. Write: "*Infinite* is the damage knowledge receives by it".

Inversion of Object. (3) *Displacement of Object.*—This again may be practised to impart emphasis to the object-word, but, on much stronger ground, to give continuity to the sentence. Even in that sentence "Silver and gold have I none", the strength lies not so much in the inversion, as in the continuity effected by inversion.

SENTENCE-GLIDES.

"*This* I thought a very preposterous beginning."

"*This temptation* he studiously avoided."

"*All these excuses*, I immediately over-ruled."

"And you realize then that, though he looks old, he must be older than he looks. *How old that is*, I could never discover."

> The Inverted object in each of these five instances introduces prominently the theme of the previous sentence; and the Inversion has consequently a connective power.

"*This*, when it was brought to him, he drank slowly like a connoisseur, lingering on the taste, and still looking about him at the cliff or up at our signboard."

> Remark here also how the sentence is compacted by inversion, the attributive phrases being brought into position with the subject "he".

The Adjective and Adjective-group. (4) *Inversion of the Adjective.*—In accordance with the *Law of Priority*, the adjectival adjunct should precede its head-word; the cases in which there is a *grammatical* perversion of this order are very few. In fact, it may be stated as a working principle of prose that the adjuncts which may *follow* the noun are not single adjectives, but

(1) a series of adjectives;

(2) adjectival or prepositional groups.

(1) *A series of adjectives.*—(i) A series of adjectives

should be arranged in the inverse order of their importance; the importance of an adjective being determined by the speciality of its application to the noun. Thus the more general should precede the more particular; *e.g.*:

His plain, green-eyed heroine; *not* His green-eyed, plain heroine.

And mere qualifiers should invariably precede attributive words; *e.g.*:

Five large beech trees.

Conversely, therefore, the attributive power of an adjective is in the direct ratio of its nearness to the noun.[1]

(ii) Inversion gives to the adjunct-words such fulness of taste as makes them almost equivalent to adjunct-clauses; *e.g.*:

Warriors *brave and true* were there.

A special fulness may be imparted to any particular adjunct by breaking the series; *e.g.*:

Brave warriors, *and true* were there.
He was an able administrator, *and an active*.

(2) *Adjectival or prepositional groups.*—An adjective-group, or a preposition-group equivalent

[1] My attention has been directed to a passage in HENRY SWEET'S *A New English Grammar* (1898), Part II., Syntax (p. 9), which seems to be at variance with this view: "When the modifiers are about equally balanced, the order may vary, as in *the two first weeks, the first two weeks*". I doubt if there can in nature be such a thing possible as adjuncts "equally balanced". Surely, the indifferent order here recorded is due to that want of precision which characterizes the colloquial language, but which is quite inadmissible in literary prose. There is in reality no conflict of opinion; Mr. SWEET'S position is that of the philologist, for whom colloquial and literary phenomena are equally valuable. He also admits the "split infinitive".

to an adjective, should precede, if it may do so
without impairing the construction; *e.g.*:

> This *ever to be remembered* victory,

but not

> "This *up to the present at any rate unrecorded* remark".
> "The fact of its having been considered advisable being *quite
> eloquent enough a* commentary."

Adjective-groups may for the sake of continuity
take front position in the sentence; they, like the
leading adverb-phrases, often serve as sentence-
glides.

SENTENCE-GLIDES.

"*Of all the beasts that graze the lawn, or hunt the forest,* a dog is the only animal that, leaving his fellows, attempts to cultivate the friendship of man."

By this inversion also, the phrase "the only animal that" is brought easily into position.

"*Studious to please, and fearing to offend,* he is still an humble, steadfast dependent."

Recapitulatory; and therefore serving merely as a 'glide'.

"*Perceiving my business,* he desired me to enter and sit down."

"*Struggling here for some time in order to be the first to see the cavalcade* as it passed, some one of the crowd unluckily happened to tread upon my shoe."

Recapitulatory, and therefore a 'sentence-glide'; moreover the participial phrase is here very heavy.

RELATIVE WORDS AND CLAUSES.

**Explicit
Reference
of Pronouns.**
By "Relative Words and Clauses" is
meant (i) *Pronouns* (he, she, it, one,
&c.) which are *not notional words*, but
borrow a meaning from some antecedent. For
them, no rule can be given except this: the reference of the words must be clearly marked by

giving prominence to the antecedent-word, and by avoiding the possibility of two antecedents. Where there is possible ambiguity, not a pronoun, but a synonymous expression must be used; or the notional word must be repeated. *E.g.* "We said to my lord, the lad cannot leave his father; for if he should leave his father, *his father* [not "he"] would die".

"However fine a sight the fleet was by day, *it* was certainly eclipsed by night."	The fleet, or the sight? For "it" write "this spectacle".
"The influence of books is similar to that of human companionship, because what we read contains the thoughts of men and women; and we extract *them* for filling our minds and enlarging our views."	Thoughts, or men and women? Write "and these thoughts we extract".
"The finest work of ages is presented to us here, and where there is the necessary taste, *it* may if not create, at least develop *it*."	Hopelessly inexplicit.
"Works of fiction give us numerous examples; but there is no necessity to apply to books, for *they* abound in everyday life."	For "they" write "such instances".
"Their father, who was a soldier, was dead; Harry said he should be *one* when he grew up."	The word "soldier", occurring as it does in a subordinate clause, is not sufficiently prominent to be referred to merely by a pronoun; say "he should be a soldier".

Reference of the Adjective-Clause. (ii) *The Adjective-clause.*—It is of first necessity to make clear the reference of the Adjective-clause to its antecedent. When there is any probable ambiguity or difficulty, a juxtaposition must be effected even by inverting the sentence.

"This kind of wit was very much in vogue among our *countrymen* about an age or two ago, *who* did not practise it for any oblique reason, but purely for the sake of being witty."

Juxtaposition is here easily to be effected by displacing the adverb-phrase: "This kind of wit was about an age or two ago very much in vogue among our *countrymen, who* . . ."

"and to have the *principles* explained to them, *on which* the argument proceeds."

Simple inversion: "and to have explained to them the *principles on which* . . ."

"or may almost affix any *meaning* to them he pleases."

Displacement of adverb-phrase: "or may almost affix to them any *meaning* he pleases."

"*Epigram* marched up in the rear, *who* had been posted there at the beginning of the expedition."

Displacement and inversion: "In the rear marched *Epigram, who* . . ."

"Those who have no intention of walking in the paths of art themselves may yet receive *help* from the works of genius they see around them, *which* will aid them in their own employment."

Displacement of adverb-phrase: " . . . may yet receive, from the works of genius they see around them, *help which* will aid . . ."

"It is folly to pretend to arm ourselves against the *accidents of life* by heaping up treasures, *which* nothing can protect us against but the good providence of our Heavenly Father."

Very ambiguous reference; write: "It is folly to pretend, by heaping up treasures, to arm ourselves against the *accidents of life, against which* nothing . . ."

"We shall hear *those things* commended and cried up for the best writings, *which* a man would scarce vouchsafe to wrap any wholesome drug in."

Reference a little ambiguous. Reconstruct as before.

When the antecedent has such prominence in the preceding sentence that no ambiguity or difficulty is possible, it is somewhat pedantic to insist on juxtaposition. Juxtaposition would, indeed, in many cases, impair the balance of the sentence. There is, however, no other consideration save *the balance of the sentence* which will excuse our not placing the relative *next* to its antecedent.

Such sentences as the following it would be inexpedient to disturb:

"How can *they* comfort or instruct others, *who* can scarce feel their own existence".

"*He* is thrice-armed, *that* hath his quarrel just."

"I warrant your grace *you* shall not entreat him to a second, *that* have so mightily persuaded him from a first."

"The *husband* had now arrived for *whom* she had waited so long."

"It is impossible for any *thought* to be beautiful *which* [that[1]] is not just."

"*Those* doubtless argued best against him *who* really disbelieved his discovery."

"*Those dogmas* are beyond the reach of cool reasoning, *which* [that[1]] are within the rightful confines of ridicule."

"*Nature* does not withhold one faculty, *who* is so prodigal of many."

The Use of "Who", "Which", and "That". The double office of the Adjective-clause (*Continuating* and *Restrictive*) has been already remarked upon (p. 30). The words *who* and *which* are naturally of the continuating or co-ordinate kind, equivalent to *and he, she . . . ; for he, she . . ., &c.*

"I gave the card to my sister, *who* (=and she) handed it to the doorkeeper."

"He said nothing; *which* (=and this) was very rude of him."

"He *that* [restrictive] beguiled you in a plain accent was a plain knave, *which* (=but this) for my part I will not be."

"Three or four loving lords have put themselves into voluntary exile with him, *whose* (=and their) lands and revenues enrich the new duke."

1 See below, p. 60.

"Nothing remains but that I kindle the boy thither, *which* (=and this) now I'll go about."

"It is worthy of remark, however, that the very same erroneous view is even now often taken of Logic; *which* (=for this) has been considered by some as a kind of system . . ."

"We had some heavy weather, *which* (=but this) only proved the qualities of the Hispaniola."

Continuating or Co-ordinate
$\begin{cases} \textit{who}\text{---referring to Persons.} \\ \textit{which}\text{---referring to Animals, Inanimate things, Abstractions.} \end{cases}$

The word 'that', however, being a purely relational word, can introduce only a clause that restricts, limits, or defines some antecedent word or phrase.

Restrictive
$\begin{cases} \textit{That}\text{---referring to Persons, Animals, Inanimate things, Abstractions.} \end{cases}$

"Those dogmas are beyond the reach of cool reasoning, *that* are within the rightful confines of ridicule."

"Those seeming resemblances or contradictions *that* make up all the wit in this kind."

"The satisfaction *that* comes from good works is lasting."

"A man may fish with the worm *that* hath eat of a king."

The restrictive nature of 'that' should never be forgotten.

I know that *all words that* are signs of complex ideas furnish matter of mistake and cavil.	"*all those words that.*"
To free his bride *that* was so dear.	'. . . *who* was so dear.' There is no restriction here.
"I found there were artificial echoes in every walk, *that*, by repetition of certain words *which* I spoke, agreed with me or contradicted me in everything I said."	"*which*, by repetition of certain words *that* I spoke."

'That' should never be employed co-ordinately; 'who' and 'which' may, however, be used restrictively under the following conditions:

(i) To avoid a weak prepositional ending; because 'that' may never be preceded by a preposition.

"should be metaphorically true of the object *that* we are speaking *of.*	of the object *of which* we are speaking.
"the very words *that* they refer *to.*"	the very words *to which* they refer.

(ii) To avoid repetition; where, in the same sentence, 'that' is employed in some one of its many other functions.

"*That* is the man *that* I saw."	*whom* I saw.
	"Bonhours . . . has taken pains to show *that* it is impossible for any thought to be beautiful, *which* is not just."
	"Rightly considering *that* prose to be best, *which* had fewest of the attributes peculiar to poetry."
"It is help of *that* kind *that* is most effective."	It is help of *that* kind, *which* is most effective.

(iii) To avoid repetition of the same pronoun, when there are several relative clauses in the sentence.

"By his own account he must have lived his life among some of the wickedest men *that* God ever allowed upon the sea; and the language in *which* he told these stories shocked our plain country people almost as much as the crimes *that* he described."

(iv) Where, in the case of co-ordinate relative

clauses, the same pronoun has to be repeated before each (see p. 63).

A Sequence of Adjective-Clauses. In this connection, it may be remarked that a long train of relative clauses should be as far as possible avoided. Not only is a sequence of relative clauses essentially inartistic, but it tends greatly to impair the unity of the sentence.

"In like manner, we frequently meet with expert artisans who are ignorant of the six mechanical powers; *which, though in the exercise of their profession they daily employ*, they do not understand the principles, whereby in any instance the result of their application is ascertained."	Break the unsightly series of relative clauses thus: *and, though in the exercise of their profession, they daily employ them,*
"Many other instances might be adduced, in which truths of the highest importance may be elicited by this process of argumentation; *which will enable us to decide* with sufficient probability what consequence would follow from an hypothesis, which we have never experienced."	*for this method will enable us to decide*, or *for it is a method that will enable us to decide*
"Another cousin, Mrs. Marie Clothilde Balfour, whose father was a son of the Colinton manse, who died young, and who is married to her cousin—a son of Dr. G. W. Balfour, who can also, like his father, write acceptably on medical and other subjects—has already gained for herself no inconsiderable repute as a novelist."	Structure quite hopeless; no artistry, and worse, no unity in the sentence. Reconstruct as follows: "Another cousin, Mrs. Marie Clothilde Balfour, has already gained for herself no inconsiderable repute as a novelist. Her father, who died young, was a son of the Colinton manse; and she is married to her cousin, Dr. G. W. Balfour's son, who can also, like his father, write acceptably on medical and other subjects."

"So much has this been the tendency in England, that we know a person of great powers, but who has in all things a one-sided taste, and is so much a lover of idiomatic English as to endure nothing else, who professes to read no writer since Lord Chesterfield."

Probably as perplexing to the writer as to the reader. Reconstruct as follows:

"So much has this been the tendency in England, that we know a person of great powers but of a one-sided taste, who can endure nothing else. He is so much a lover of idiomatic English that he professes to read no writer since Lord Chesterfield."

A train of adjective-clauses is chiefly useful for the effect of climax.

"They only collect their materials from the oracle of some coffee-house, *which oracle* has himself gathered them the night before from a beau at a gaming-table, *who* has pillaged his knowledge from a great man's porter, *who* has had his information from the great man's gentleman, *who* has invented the whole story for his own amusement the night preceding."

Co-ordinate Adjective-Clauses. When there are several adjective-clauses to the *same antecedent*, they should be co-ordinated by conjunctions, and the same pronoun should be repeated before each.[1]

"The man, *that* we observed in the hall, *who* is intimately associated with the movement . . ."

The man, *whom* we observed in the hall, *and who* is intimately . . .

"The different bodies of forces, *which* I had before seen in the temple, *who* were drawn up in battle-array . . . "

The different bodies of forces, *which* I had before seen in the temple, *and which* were drawn up in battle-array . . .

[1] It is necessary to repeat the connective, *in all cases* where subordinate clauses are co-ordinated with each other. The following is an example of Co-ordinated Noun-clauses:

"He owned, when driven into a corner, *that* he seemed to have been wrong about the crew, *that* some of them were as brisk as he wanted to see, *and* all had behaved fairly well."

and that

"There is another kind of wit *which* consists partly in the resemblance of ideas, and partly in the resemblance of words, *which* for distinction sake I shall call mixt wit."

and which

"At this triumph we were filled with hope, and hurried upstairs without delay to the little room, *where* he had slept so long, *and where* his box had stood since the day of his arrival."

Care must be had lest the adjective-clause be *falsely* co-ordinated with some phrase or with a clause not adjectival; the conjunctions *and, but,* &c., may never be employed before a relative pronoun, except to co-ordinate it with a preceding relative pronoun.

FALSELY CO-ORDINATED CLAUSES.

"Again, there was the subject of his relations with his mother, *which* were now upon an equable and peaceful but never confidential footing; *and whom* he saw several times a week."

Two clauses referring to different antecedents—"relations" and "mother"—are here co-ordinated by means of "and". For "and whom . . ." write "*her* he saw several times a week".

"Though a favourable environment does not necessarily elevate the character of the individual, yet the persons whose characters are not elevated are only the exceptions to the rule, *and who* have the opposite qualities strongly inherited."

The adjective-clause is here falsely co-ordinated with the principal sentence itself; for "and who" say *and those who,* or simply *who.*

"Children from very squalid homes, *or who* have criminal parents, . . ."

A very common form of the error. The adjective-clause is co-ordinated with a mere phrase—"from very squalid homes". Say "who come from very squalid homes, or who have criminal parents".

"He was a man of great refinement, *and who* seemed to enjoy . . ."	Omit "and", or say "and one who".
"A gentleman, said to be a correspondent of the London Star, *and who* was fighting among the Garibaldians, was killed."	Omit "and".
"A nation is an object more important, *and which* fills the mind with a grander idea than a private individual."	Omit "and"; or write "and one which".
"One can understand the feeling so common among De Quincey's admirers of former years, *and which* still sometimes finds expression . . ."	"the feeling *which was* so common among De Quincey's admirers of former years, *and which* still sometimes finds expression . . ."
"Refinement in writing expresses a less natural and obvious train of thought, *and which* it requires a peculiar turn of genius to pursue."	"which" is in itself a connective, and requires no "and" save to co-ordinate it with a preceding "which". Write "obvious train of thought *which* it requires . . ."
"Colonel Sandys, a hot man, *and who* had more courage than judgment."	Omit "and".

The same type of error is exhibited in the following constructions:

FALSELY CO-ORDINATED.

The powers they possess but cannot make use of *them*.	The adjective-clause "they possess" is joined by "but" to a simple sentence. Write: "The powers which they possess, but of which they cannot make use"; or more rapid form: "the powers they possess, but cannot make use of".
"In the afternoon the old gentleman proposed a walk to Vauxhall, a place *of which* he had heard much, *but* had never seen *it*."	"*of which* he had heard much, *but which* he had never seen."

RAPIDITY OF STYLE.

Omission of the Relative. The Relative may be omitted where it is desirable to give rapidity to the style, *e.g.*:

"May affix to them almost any meaning   he pleases".

"the great folk   you saw passing by just now."

"The most improper things   we commit in the course of our lives we are led into by the force of fashion."

"the grief   we have for the loss of our friends."

"too much distressed to take the care   they ought of their dress."

Participial Phrase. For the sake of rapidity, it is frequently expedient to substitute a participial phrase, for adjective clauses, for adverb clauses of all kinds, and even for co-ordinate sentences.

"at his heels a rabble of his companions, thither *provoked and instigated* by his distemper."	for *adjective - clause* "who were thither provoked. . . ."
"I fear he will prove the weeping philosopher when he grows old, *being* so full of unmannerly sadness in his youth."	*Causal.*
"You have trained me like a peasant, *obscuring* and *hiding* from me all gentlemanlike qualities."	*Causal.*
"*Finding* ourselves slow of sail, we put on a compelled valour."	*Temporal* or *Causal.*
"The wall, methinks, *being* sensible, should curse again."	*Causal.*
"the duke's daughter, her cousin, so loves her, *being* ever from their cradles bred together, that . . ."	*Causal.*
"Alas, poor shepherd, *searching* of thy wound, I have by hard adventure found mine own."	*Temporal* or *Instrumental.*
"Yonder is a most reverend gentleman, who, belike, *having* received wrong by some person, is at most odds with his own gravity and patience that ever you saw."	*Causal.*

"But, *being* desirous to get out of this world of magic, which had almost turned my brain, I left the temple."	*Causal* = "as I was".
"The periods of such a prose can never be artificial, *being* contrived according to the natural ideal of every man that wishes simply and clearly to show forth the heads of his meaning."	*Causal* = "because they are".
"Cowley, *observing* the cold regard of his mistress' eyes, and at the same time their power of producing love in him, considers them as burning glasses made of ice; and, *finding* himself able to live in the greatest extremities of love, concludes the Torrid Zone to be habitable."	*Temporal* "when he observes", "when he finds".
"I look upon these writers as Goths in poetry, who, like those in architecture, not *being* able to come up to the beautiful simplicity of the old Greeks and Romans, have endeavoured to supply its place with all the extravagancies of an irregular fancy."	*Causal* or *Temporal* "since they are unable", or "when they are unable".

The frequent expediency of the Participial Phrase will be abundantly apparent from the above examples. Contrast also the following:

SLOW.	RAPID.
This letter *was written* without any dot, *and so* was liable to be mistaken for a part of another letter.	This letter, *being written* without any dot, was liable to be mistaken for a part of another letter.
I made the best of my way upstairs; *but had* lost so much blood, *that* I had hardly spirits enough to keep me from swooning.	I made the best of my way upstairs; *but, having lost* so much blood, I had hardly spirits enough to keep me from swooning.

Care must be had, however, to determine exactly the reference of the participle. A ludicrous picture is here presented:

"A road is cut through it, and walking along on both sides are the rocks, towering up, covered with trees, shrubs, ferns, and heather".

(M 544) E

III. THE USE OF STOPS.

"The very nature of speech, because it goeth by clauses of several construction and sense, requireth some space betwixt them with intermission of sound, to the end they may not huddle one upon another so rudely and so fast that the ear may not perceive their difference" (GEORGE PUTTENHAM, *The Arte of English Poesie*).

The Office of Punctuation. Pause, stress, and modulation, play so important a part in the spoken language, that some adequate substitute is indispensable in the written language. Only by properly 'pointing' or 'stopping' our written discourse are we enabled to group our words and phrases together, to mark the *intermissions of sound*, to indicate the *quantity* of the sentence, and to prevent ambiguity. For this purpose we have in English four pause-marks: (1) *Comma* (,), (2) *Semi-colon* (;), (3) *Colon* (:), (4) *Full-stop* (.).

The Uses of the Comma. RULE I.—ANY WORD, PHRASE, OR CLAUSE THAT BREAKS THE THREAD OF THE MAIN STATEMENT MUST BE SEPARATED OUT BY COMMAS.

The word, phrase, or clause (*a*) may be obviously parenthetical:

"This, all things considered, is a good plan".
"Every day, when he came back from his stroll, he would ask if any seafaring man had gone by along the road."

or (*b*) it may be isolated from the principal sentence:

"When the idol had done speaking, I concluded the service was over".

No phrase or clause is isolated in the sentence except for emphasis; 'pointing' enforces the isolation, and consequently the emphasis.

Particular Applications of this Rule. (i) *The Adverb-phrase or Adverb-clause.*—When the adverbial qualification is short, and follows the principal assertion, no pause is required in speaking and no comma in writing:

" The audience was seated when the music began ".

" The audience was seated in the open air."

" We require to observe the context in order thoroughly to appreciate the passage."

" Our case seemed so hopeless that we gave ourselves up to despair."

But when (*a*) either the principal or the subsidiary statement is long, or (*b*) when the adverbial qualification intrudes into or (*c*) prefaces the principal sentence—then there are distinct intermissions of sound in speaking, and in writing commas are required:

(*a*) " Not even the Kalmucks would be guilty of such an indecency, though all the object of their worship was but a joint stool ".

(*b*) " This, if I am not greatly mistaken, is an utterly false statement of the case."

(*c*) " When he began to speak, all the people remained fixed in silent attention."

" As he fancied himself quite unperceived, he continued to rail against me."

" In order to appreciate the passage, we require to observe the context."

If the adverbial phrase is short, no comma is needed, though it preface the sentence:

" In the end he consented ".

Further, where the verb is inverted the qualifying phrase is not pointed, because it is then in
juxtaposition with the predicate.

Compare:

| Down the long avenue, the great house of the squire lay. | Down the long avenue lay the great house of the squire. |

(ii) *The Adjective Phrase or Clause.*

The Adjective-phrase, unless parenthetical, or displaced from the word or phrase that it qualifies,
requires no pointing.

At the top of the field lay a house surrounded with trees.

But remark:

| He was an able administrator, and an active. He went everywhere, shadowed and watched. | Displaced. |

If the Adjective-phrase preface the sentence, it
requires pointing:

"Turning to another part of the temple, I perceived a young
lady just in the same circumstances and attitude".

or if it be a long phrase closing the sentence:

"He began to examine the sailor, demanding in what engage-
ment he was thus disabled".

The Adjective-clause, when it is of a restrictive
nature, requires no comma; but, when it is used
continuatively, it must be 'pointed' out:

| "The idol *that* they seem to address strides like a colossus over the door of the inner temple, *which* here, as with the Jews, is esteemed the most sacred part of the building." | The restrictive *that*-clause requires no comma; the *which*-clause, introducing an independent co-ordinate statement, must be pointed. |

Further, if the adjective-clause is displaced, it requires a comma:

"He is thrice armed, that hath his quarrel just".

(iii) *The Noun Phrase or Clause.—The Noun-phrase*, occurring in its grammatical order, as subject, object, or complement, requires no comma:

To speak with importance and dignity upon trifles requires a special training.	The subject is in its grammatical order.
He readily grasped the difference between example and advice.	The object is in its grammatical order.

But when the subject is delayed, or the object brought to the front of the sentence, commas are necessary:

"It requires a special training, to speak with importance and dignity upon trifles."	Subject delayed.
"The difference between example and advice, he readily grasped."	Object displaced.

The Noun-clause—

(*a*) *as subject.* If it precedes the predicate, no comma is required, the connection between subject and predicate being too close to admit of 'pointing':

"That you have wronged me doth appear in this".

But, if the noun-clause is suspended, a comma is necessary; because the clause is, by suspension, displaced in the sentence.

"In this doth it appear, that you have wronged me."

(*b*) *as object.* Similarly, when the object-clause follows the predicate, no comma is required; but if it precedes, it should be 'stopped':

"I am certain that you are wrong".
"That you are wrong, I am certain."

(*c*) *as complement.* The Noun-clause as complement never requires pointing, because its displacement invariably involves inversion of the predicate:

"The contention was that he had made a disastrous blunder".	"That he had made a disastrous blunder was the contention."

(*d*) *in apposition.* If it be restrictive in force,
no comma is necessary:

"The reason why he asked me was quite apparent".

But if it be continuative, it should be separated out
by commas:

"My simple remark, that he had proved himself inconsistent,
excited much displeasure".

If it is displaced from the word with which it
agrees, it should always be separated by a comma:

"The question was asked, why he had not come earlier".

(iv) There are some usages, *invariably paren-*
thetical, that require pointing by means of commas:

(*a*) Words or phrases of a connective nature
intruding into the sentence:

"But this, perhaps, is not a good example".
"You, however, should know this."
"He, in any case, will be found willing."
"The secretary, consequently, tendered his resignation."

(*b*) Short parenthetical sentences (if the parentheses are long, use brackets or the dash):

"This, I believe, is a true statement of the case".
"'This armour', said he, 'belonged to General Monk.'"
"The man who, they thought, had committed the theft."

In this last example, remark that, by properly stopping the parenthetical sentence 'they thought', the fact of the parenthesis is emphasized, and there is no temptation to subordinate to the parenthetical sentence the nominative *who*, as in the vulgar error, "*whom* they thought had committed the theft".

(c) A phrase added by way of alternative or qualification:

"Such women generally marry men as young as, or even younger than, themselves".

"The spirit of the discourse, and indeed the letter also, was contrary to his principles."

"Popular humour, or party spirit, may at other times exalt to a high, though short-lived, reputation what little deserves it."

(d) Nominative of address:

"Mostadad, O my father, is no philosopher".
"Lord, my dear, you seem immensely chagrined."

(e) Where a word or phrase is iterated:

"Fallen, fallen is Babylon the great."
"It was a weary, weary way."

RULE II.—THE COMMA IS USED TO INDICATE ELLIPSIS, IF AMBIGUITY IS POSSIBLE.

"There fluttered a sheet of manuscript; there, a torn handkerchief."

But if there is no possible ambiguity, such pointing is unnecessary, because there is no intermission of sound in speaking.

"Elizabeth betrayed her enemies; Mary her friends."

RULE III.—THE COMMA IS USED TO SEPARATE
WORDS, PHRASES, OR CLAUSES, WHEN THEY OCCUR
IN SERIES.

"The poor are here supplied with food, clothes, fire, and a
bed to lie on."

"They make use of music to warm their hearts, and to lift
them to a proper pitch of rapture."

"These are countries from whence the rigorous climate, the
sweeping inundation, the drifted desert, the howling forest, and
mountains of immeasurable height banish the husbandman."

In this last example, it will be remarked that no
point is placed after "mountains of immeasurable
height". In such a series a climax is generally
intended; to pause at the last word mars the climax.
Remark also:

"He was an astute, active, and dangerous man".

So also in the case of verbal iteration, the climax
is assisted by the omission of the last comma:

"Fallen, fallen is Babylon the great".

If no climax is intended, a comma should be used
at the end of the series:

"Good sense, clear ideas, perspicuity of language, and proper
arrangement of words and thoughts, will always command
attention".

If the series consists merely of two words joined
by a conjunction, the comma is unnecessary:

"He was an able and active administrator".
"He was everywhere shadowed and watched."

When the conjunction is omitted, the comma should
be used:

"He was an able, active administrator".

When the series consists of a word and a phrase the comma is necessary; ambiguity is otherwise possible:

"I saw a man, and a dog led by a chain".

"He was everywhere shadowed, and watched by the keen eye of the law."

Finally, a series of short co-ordinate sentences connected by conjunctions may be separated by commas:

"He can read, but he cannot write".

"He has only had the misfortune of eating too hearty a meal, and finds it impossible to keep his eyes open."

But if the co-ordinate sentences are long or complex in themselves, or unconnected by conjunctions, they must be divided by the *semi-colon*.

The Uses of the Semi-colon. THE SEMI-COLON IS PRIMARILY THE CO-ORDINATE-SENTENCE STOP. It must be employed—

(i) When the co-ordinate sentences, though short, are unconnected by conjunctions:

"To spend too much time in studies is sloth; to use them too much for ornament is affectation; to make judgment wholly by their rules is the humour of a scholar".

(ii) When the co-ordinate sentences are long or complex:

"He readily believed them; the guardians of the temple, as they got by the self-delusion, were ready to believe him too; so he paid his money for a fine monument; and the workman, as you see, has made him one of the most beautiful".

Since the comma is employed for its special purposes within these co-ordinate sentences, we must
necessarily rise at the close of each to a semi-colon.

Similarly, when clauses, or even phrases, are so
long or complicated as to require the use of commas
within themselves; they must be separated from
each other, or from the principal statement, by the
semi-colon:

"These answerers have no other employment but to cry out
Dunce and Scribbler; to praise the dead, and revile the living;
to grant a man of confessed abilities some small share of merit;
to applaud twenty blockheads in order to gain the reputation of
candour; and to revile the moral character of the man whose
writings they cannot injure".

"Such wretches are kept in pay by some mercenary bookseller,
or more frequently the bookseller himself takes this dirty work
off their hands; as all that is required is to be very abusive and
very dull."

"I was surprised at such a demand, and asked the man
whether the people of England kept a show; whether the paltry
sum he demanded was not a national reproach; whether it was
not more to the honour of the country to let their magnificence
or their antiquities be openly seen, than thus meanly to tax a
curiosity which tended to their own honour."

**The Uses of
the Colon.** Example:

"Your wife, daughter, and the rest of your
family have been seized by his order, and appropriated to his
use; all, except your son, are now the peculiar property of him
who possesses all: him I have hidden from the officers employed
for this purpose; and, even at the hazard of my life, I have concealed him".

(i) In the above sentence, the first two co-ordinate
statements refer to the fate of a whole family; the
last two to the fate of a single member of the
family. At the phrase *possesses all*, there is a

longer intermission than anywhere else; the whole sentence falling into two distinct, though related, parts. In a series of *co-ordinate statements*, it frequently happens that some will so group together that the pause following them is more prolonged than any pause occurring between the individual statements themselves. A special intermission of this kind is pointed by a *colon*.

(ii) Again, we frequently meet with co-ordinate statements that are purely illustrative, explanatory, or enumerative. These should invariably be prefaced by a *colon*, which is here equivalent to *viz., namely*.

"You see, my dearest friend, what imprudence has brought thee to: from opulence, a tender family, surrounding friends, and your master's esteem, it has reduced thee to want, persecution, and, still worse, to our mighty monarch's displeasure."

"I now looked round me as directed, but saw nothing of that fervent devotion which he had promised: one of the worshippers appeared to be ogling the company through a glass; another was fervent, not in addresses to Heaven, but to his mistress; a third whispered; a fourth took snuff; and the priest himself, in a drowsy tone, read over the *duties* of the day."

Milton was the author of the following works: *Paradise Lost, Paradise Regained, Samson Agonistes*, and *Comus*.

(iii) It follows, therefore, that a direct quotation prefaced by *he said, he answered*, or the like, must be introduced by a *colon*. The quotation in such a case must be placed between *inverted commas*[1] ("......"); *e.g.*:

Truly has Froude remarked: "Of all powers of evil in high places, there is none equal for the mischief which it can produce to incapacity".

1 Where a quotation is placed within a quotation, double commas are used without ("....") and single commas within ('....').

If we insert parenthetically the reference to the writer, we shall point thus:

"Of all powers of evil in high places," remarks Mr. Froude, "there is none equal for the mischief which it can produce to incapacity".

If the quotation be indirect (oblique oration), it becomes a noun-clause, and no such pointing is required; *e.g.*:

Froude has remarked that, of all powers of evil in high places, there is none equal for the mischief which it can produce to incapacity.

A citation which forms part of the body of the statement requires no colon; *e.g.*:

Froude, speaking of the powers of evil in high places, remarks that "there is none equal for the mischief which it can produce to incapacity".

The Uses of the Full-stop. "The third they called *periodus*, for a complement or full pause, and as a resting-place and perfection of so much former speech as had been uttered, and from whence they needed not to pass any further, unless it were to renew more matter to enlarge the tale." [PUTTEN-HAM.]

The *Full-stop*, in addition to pointing a "full pause" at the close of a completed sentence, is also used to mark abbreviations: M.A.; *i.e.*; viz.; Dr. E. H. Scott; 130 B.C. The full-stop pointing abbreviations does not preclude the use of any other stop immediately following, unless the following stop be another full-stop.

"Oliver Jones, B.A., on rising to speak, betrayed some trepidation."

The Note of Interrogation. THE NOTE OF INTERROGATION IS USED AFTER A DIRECT QUESTION.

> Who is there?

When the question is *indirect*, it becomes a noun-clause; and no note of interrogation is required.

> He asked who was there.

The Note of Interrogation is equivalent to a full-stop, and must therefore mark a "full pause": it cannot intrude into the middle of a sentence.

> "Yet why wish for his wealth, with his ignorance; to be like him incapable of sentimental pleasures?"

A series of co-ordinate questions requires a Note of Interrogation only at the close or " full pause ".

> "Why was I brought into being; for what purposes made; from whence have I come; whither strayed; or to what regions am I hastening?"

A rhetorical question, since it demands no explicit answer, is usually pointed by a *note of exclamation.*

> "Must every luxury of the great be woven from the calamities of the poor!"

Note of Exclamation. THE NOTE OF EXCLAMATION POINTS WORDS, PHRASES, AND SENTENCES OF AN EXCLAMATORY NATURE.

> "Into what a state of misery are the modern Persians fallen!"
> "Genius of the sun! What unexpected softness! What animated grace!"

The *Note of Exclamation* marks, as does the note of interrogation, a full pause. It must always be succeeded by a capital letter, and should not intrude into the middle of a sentence. We may write:

"Heavens! How much is requisite to make one man happy!"

or better

"Heavens, how much is requisite to make one man happy!"

We may not write

"Heavens! how much is requisite to make one man happy!"

An exclamatory word or phrase in the body of the sentence should be pointed with commas.

"Mostadad, O my father, is no philosopher."

A series of co-ordinate exclamations requires pointing only at the close.

First blast me to the centre; degrade me beneath the most degraded; pare my nails, ye powers of Heaven, ere I would stoop to such an exchange!"

A point of exclamation frequently enforces the irony, or the absurdity, or the dignity of a thought. If, however, the idea is not intrinsically impressive, or absurd, or ironical, no such pointing will make it so.

The Dash. When an important part of the sentence is so long or involved that its bearing might be lost, it is permissible to use a *dash*.

"To study and to know our own genius well; to follow nature; to seek to improve, but not to force it—are directions which cannot be too often given to those who desire to excel in the liberal arts."

The dash is most commonly used, as in the above example, to close a heavy subject. If the subject is not too heavy, we may use a comma.

"But the combination of the forms of chivalrous devotion with the reality of cynical contempt, was the peculiar tone of manners. . . ."

The dash is also used to mark

(a) Hesitation.

"Well—h'm—yes—yes—that is so."

(b) An abrupt change of structure.

"Next morning he went away to—no, I shall not say where."

(c) A parenthetical sentence (instead of brackets).

"The honest hands—and I was soon to see it proved that there were such on board—must have been very stupid fellows."

(d) A phrase, illustrative, enumerative, or explanatory; where the dash is equivalent to viz., namely (instead of the colon).

"We now turn to something that, we are sure, will prove of interest to our readers—the state of England in 1685."

IV. THE NATURE OF SENTENCES.

Sentence-Length. It is impossible to prescribe definite rules for sentence-length. The short sentence engages; the long sentence holds the attention. The short sentence is more easily comprehended and remembered; the long sentence is adapted to detail, and to the amplification of the sense. The

short sentence is suited to passages of definition
and discrimination, to the critical points in a theme,
to passages of insistence; the long sentence serves
to group related facts, to secure a climax. But
even when the student has realized all this, he is
still without a definite working principle. The
habit acquired by deliberate personal investigation
of prose-style will provide an instinct that is more
valuable than a rule. It is nevertheless of great
importance that he should, from the first, realize
the absolute necessity of *variety* in the kind of
sentences he employs. This continual change of
tone, both in regard to the *length*, and also in regard
to the *nature* of sentences (*balanced, loose, periodic,*
and so forth), constitutes the native harmony of
English prose.

(i) "In respect to the construction of sentences,
it is an obvious caution to abstain from such as are
too long; but it is a mistake to suppose that the
obscurity of many long sentences depends on their
length alone. A well-constructed sentence of very
considerable length may be more readily understood
than a shorter one which is more awkwardly framed.
If a sentence be so constructed that the meaning of
each part can be taken in as we proceed (though it
be evident that the sense is not brought to a close),
its length will be little or no impediment to perspicuity; but, if the former part of the sentence
convey no distinct meaning till we arrive nearly at
the end (however plain it may then appear), it will
be on the whole deficient in perspicuity: for it will
need to be read over, or *thought over*, a second time,

in order to be fully comprehended; which is what few readers or hearers are willing to be burdened with."—ARCHBISHOP WHATELY.

(ii) "But, in almost every kind of composition, *the great rule is to intermix them.* For the ear tires of either of them when too long continued; whereas, by a proper mixture of long and short periods, the ear is gratified, and a certain sprightliness is joined with majesty in our style."—ARCHBISHOP WHATELY.

Sentence-Resolution. But, over and above this intermixture of long and short periods, in every great piece of prose, change of tone is effected also by continual *resolutions* of the *form* of the sentence.

The structure of our English sentence is essentially co-ordinate; but the staccato effect of a series of co-ordinate sentences should be carefully modified by periodic resolutions, especially at the close:

"I shall do my friends no wrong, for I have none to lament me; the world no injury, for in it I have nothing: only in the world I fill a place, *which may be better supplied, when I have made it empty*".

"Why, look you now, how unworthy a thing you make of me: you would play upon me; you would seem to know my stops; you would pluck out the heart of my mystery; you would sound me from the lowest note to the top of my compass; and there is much music, excellent voice in this little organ, yet you cannot make it speak: 's blood, do you think *I am easier to be played on than a pipe? Call me what instrument you will, though you fret me, you cannot play upon me.*"

Loose and Periodic Structure. The nature of sentences, irrespective of length, is twofold. The difference lies in the manner of laying down the main proposition.

(i) If the main proposition is despatched early, and followed by subsidiary phrases and clauses, or by co-ordinate elements amplifying it, the structure of the sentence may be described in general terms as *Loose*.

(ii) If, on the other hand, the main proposition is ushered in by subsidiary phrases or clauses, in such a manner that the essential subject of thought is suspended to the close, the sentence takes the *Periodic* form.

LOOSE.	PERIODIC.
" This rural politeness is very troublesome to a man of my temper, who generally take the chair that is next me, and walk first or last, in the front or in the rear, as chance directs."	"To a man of my temper, who generally take the chair that is next me, and walk first or last, in the front or in the rear, as chance directs, *this rural politeness is very troublesome.*"

To what an extent phrases or clauses may be delayed or suspended in the sentence has already been determined in the section on Sentence Structure. It has already been seen that, when subordinate circumstances are to be stated, the periodic structure is often inevitable, in order that the 'capital' phrase in the sentence may stand clear. This general maxim of Blair's is very true in this regard: "any phrase, which expresses a circumstance only, always brings up the rear of a sentence with a bad grace".

It is, however, very difficult to avoid prolixity and intricacy in a sustained periodic style. It is not possible to render easy the dependence of many clauses upon one and the same principal proposition.

Consequently, it is better in a long sentence to divide the main proposition into co-ordinate parts, and thus to distribute the weight of the subordinate clauses. In this *loose-resolved* sentence (consisting of co-ordinate sentences of a complex nature), the native harmony of English prose resides.

PERIODIC SENTENCE.	LOOSE-RESOLVED SENTENCE.
" Howsoever I cannot escape from some the imputation of sharpness, but that they will say I have taken a pride or lust to be bitter, and not my youngest infant but hath come into the world with all his teeth, I would ask of these supercilious politics what nation, society, or general order or state I have provoked."	From some I cannot escape the imputation of sharpness; they will say that I have taken a pride or lust to be bitter, and that even my youngest infant hath come into the world with all his teeth : of these supercilious politics, however, I would ask, what nation, society, or general order or state I have provoked.
" But my special aim being to put the snaffle in their mouths that cry out, We never punish vice in our interludes, &c., I took the more liberty, though not without some lines of example drawn even in the ancients themselves, the goings-out of whose comedies are not always joyful, but ofttimes the bawds, servants, yea, and the masters are mulcted; and fitly, it being the office of a comic poet to imitate justice and instruct to life as well as purity of language, or stir up gentle affections : to which I shall take the occasion elsewhere to speak." [*Adjunct after full close.*]	But I took the more liberty, because my special aim was to put the snaffle in their mouths that cry out ' We never punish vice in our interludes, &c.'; in this regard I followed some lines of example drawn even in the ancients themselves, the goings-out of whose comedies are not always joyful, ofttimes the bawds, servants, yea and the masters being mulcted : and fitly so, for it is the office of a comic poet to imitate justice and instruct to life, as well as purity of language, or stir up gentle affections. To this I shall take the occasion elsewhere to speak.
" If the country gentlemen get into this infamous piece of good breeding, which reigns among the coxcombs of the town, but which has not yet made its way into the country,	This infamous piece of good-breeding, which reigns among the coxcombs of the town, has not yet made its way into the country ; and, as it is impossible for such an irrational way of

PERIODIC SENTENCE.	LOOSE-RESOLVED SENTENCE.
as it is impossible for such an irrational way of conversation to last long among a people that make any profession of religion or show of modesty, they will certainly be left in the lurch."	conversation to last long among a people that make any profession of religion or show of modesty, if the country gentlemen get into it, they will certainly be left in the lurch.

One of the perils of the *Loose* form of sentence is the accumulation of connective particles (*Polysyndeton*). It is remarkable that a connective has actually a separative force; by the suppression of connectives (*Asyndeton*) the real connection between sentences or the parts of a sentence often becomes closer.

Connectives add special weight and distinction to terms and sentences, thus:

"Truth and honour and justice were at stake".
"and chase
Anguish and doubt and fear and sorrow and pain
From mortal or immortal minds."

"Of all the parts of speech the conjunctions are the most unfriendly to vivacity" (*Campbell*). Unless, therefore, it be expedient to clog the motion of a sentence, polysyndeton should be avoided. In ordinary prose, the writer should aim at rapidity of movement, and avoid an excess of connectives, as in conversation he would avoid the excessive use of the vulgar *and so*.

Balanced Structure. (i) *Balanced Form.*—The *form*, or phraseology, of a sentence should be balanced, where there is a natural balance in the *thought*. A nice observance of this *balance of thought* is one of the characteristics of a correct and careful style; and one of the worst features in the beginner's theme arises from a defective perception of it.

A sentence is balanced in regard to its *form*, when the parts of it are made similar, in order to correspond exactly to this balance of thought; as will appear from the following examples:

BALANCE DEFECTIVE.	BALANCE CORRECT.
	In the case of two such alternatives, as are here presented, the sense imperiously demands a balanced structure:
"Fiction generally falls under two classes: either it must be an imaginary portrayal formed in the mind of the author; *or the character-sketches must be taken from life.*"	Fiction generally falls under two classes: either it must be an imaginary portrayal formed in the mind of the author; *or it must consist of character-sketches taken from life.*
"He grew up selfish and ignorant, *with base desires.*"	He grew up selfish, and ignorant, *and base in his desires.*
"Art-galleries are of no use, unless the paintings *are not only drawn well and in proportion; but there must be some life portrayed in their features and their figure.*"	Art-galleries are of no use, unless the paintings *have not only good drawing and good proportion, but have also some life portrayed in their features and their figure.*
"What we profess to despise, *we are always loth to confute.*"	What we profess to despise, *we scorn to confute.*
"These, though later in their appearing, *advance more rapidly.*"	These, though later in their appearing, *are more rapid in their advancement.*
"The peace that Walpole sought was not the peace of the country, *but that his own administration should be at peace.*"	The peace that Walpole sought was not the peace of the country, *but the peace of his own administration.*
"I may be suspected of setting up a new school of poetry, *instead of a feeble attempt to imitate the old.*"	I may be suspected of setting up a new school of poetry, *instead of feebly attempting to imitate the old.*

The student should constantly be alert to the

perception of this balance, or correspondence, in the
thoughts he has to express. He should recognize
the clearness, which is always imparted to a passage, by setting *this* against *that*. At the same
time, he should be careful not to indulge that
continual *Anthithesis* ("the invariable *this* set off
by the invariable *that*"), which is so irritating a
feature in the writing of some of our early prose-
men; *e.g.*:

> "it borrows just so much of classic costume, it employs just so
> much of antique allusion, as dignify without encumbering, and,
> without disguising, adorn; and it preserves the accents of grief
> unsilenced by the chords of poesy, the chords of poesy unjarred
> by the accents of grief"; *and so forth.*

(ii) *Balanced Order.*—When the rules of grammatical order are closely adhered to, all the parts
of a sentence, principal and subordinate, will be
found parallel in their structure. This balanced
or parallel structure may be represented by the
formula—

$$a \qquad b \qquad | \qquad a \qquad b$$

e.g.:

"She was shown into the breakfast parlour,	where all but Jane were assembled".
a *b*	*a* *b*
"His profession qualified him,	his disposition led him to talk."
a *b*	*a* *b*
"Folly often goes beyond her bounds,	but Ignorance knows none."
a *b*	*a* *b*

When, however, either in the principal part, or in
any of the subordinate parts, or in any one of the
co-ordinate elements of a sentence, *Inversion* takes

place, we have that *Crossed Balance,* which is one of the musical discords of prose:

or

The *occasional use* of this structure has two advantages: (i) the musical effect gained by relieving the perpetual harmony of the balanced structure[1]; (ii) the intellectual advantage of connecting two related phrases of the sentence closely together; *e.g.*:

" According to what the Lord commanded | so did he ".
a *b* | *b* *a*

"Though he shared the sentiments | their reasoning he frequently
of many great thinkers, | misapprehended."
a *b* | *b* *a*

"In some things, I dissent | whose wit, industry, diligence, and
from others | judgment, I look up at and admire."
b *a* | *b* *a*

"In this city stands the house | where Shakespeare lived."
b *a* | *a* *b*

CHAPTER III.

THE PARAGRAPH.

The Discipline of the Paragraph. A perfect paragraph contains one outstanding topic, to which every separate proposition must stand in some well-defined relation; in such a manner that the thought of the paragraph should be capable of

---

[1] Compare the effect of *Crossed Alliteration* in our Old-English verse-system, and in the alliterative system of the Elizabethan euphuists.

being abstracted in a single sentence. To exhibit fully the various ways in which a paragraph may grow round this essential topic, would involve a treatise upon systems of human thought. For the progress and development of a true paragraph is intimately dependent upon the logical progress and development of thought. All that may be attempted in a treatise of prose is, from the examination of a few dominant paragraph-types, to draw conclusions as to how best the integrity of the paragraph —its unity and continuity—may be maintained.

The fact of first importance, then, in regard to the paragraph is its *Unity*. This quality it is that the beginner in prose is most apt to impair. He sets down his thoughts in the order in which they occur to him, without regard to their relation to some definite central idea.

The following is a characteristic example of the common type of paragraph occurring in the student's essay. It starts topics at every step, pursues none systematically, but progresses with a zigzag motion which eludes every attempt at pursuit:

The death of Mr. Gladstone removes one of the most illustrious figures that have adorned the present century. He has played a very important part in the world's history during the Queen's long reign, and *his decease moves people to study his life and recall his achievements.* The Liberal party has lost in him their greatest leader, and though he retired from the position of being their official head four years ago, they still looked up to him for guidance and support. When Lord Rosebery took his somewhat abrupt departure, they were in the unfortunate

Here we seem to lay hold on a definite paragraph-subject, which, however, the writer follows but for one sentence.

Then he is suddenly turned by a fresh scent:

position of having no one worthily to fill the vacant post. Harcourt would have liked to step into the vacated shoes, and assume the reins of leadership [*confused metaphor*]; he, however, with all his gifts, is no Gladstone. Mr. Gladstone was not only a great statesman, but an author. When he relinquished the premiership, and severed his active connection with politics in 1894, being then in his eighty-fifth year, he became very assiduous in his literary and other work. At his great age it was most remarkable to see him so active and eager for work. He kept at his labours faithfully and cheerfully until he could do so no longer. He showed how it was possible to unite with gifts of statesmanship and oratory deep uprightness of character; and he succeeded in keeping this union intact through his long public career. All that he did was done, because he thought it to be right. This is where his chief charm lay; and this is what made him trusted and respected, even by those who widely differed from him in political and religious matters. His name will live in history for ages to come, and his memory will be cherished by all.

the state of the Liberal party at Gladstone's retirement.

The topic of statesmanship is suddenly abandoned after being scarcely broached.

Still another topic intervening: remarkable display of octogenarian energy.

Another new topic: Gladstone the man as distinct from Gladstone the statesman and author.

Every paragraph should be exhaustive of the particular view it takes of a definite topic. By massing together a number of different subjects in the same paragraph, a writer invariably obscures from himself the fact that he is *writing about none.* If he divides them into separate paragraphs, he will immediately perceive that he has merely started a topic, but has not pursued it. In the above paragraph the writer gathers together heterogeneously, in the following order, *five* different topics:

(*a*) People moved to recall the life and achievements of Gladstone.

(*b*) Rosebery, Harcourt, and the state of the Liberal Party.

(c) Gladstone, the author.
(d) His octogenarian energy.
(e) Gladstone, the man.

There is no attempt to focus these diverse topics upon one central idea; they are merely cast together pell-mell, heads of subjects with no body to them.

Again, the student will often, after having treated with some fulness and consequence of one topic, violently attack another, and leave this unfinished, to the complete ruin of the paragraph-unity. Thus, at the end of a paragraph on "the influence of human companionship upon character", we find adjoined the following:

"Books also play a great part in shaping the character. Their influence is similar to that of human companionship, because what we read contains the thoughts of men and women, and we extract them for filling our minds and enlarging our views."

This is identical in its effect to the adjunct added after the full close of a sentence. But it is even more pernicious in the case of the paragraph, because it conceals from the writer the fact that he has, after starting a topic, abandoned it while still in an undeveloped condition.

To each new head in the essay must be allotted a separate paragraph. Where this is done, the writer immediately perceives those parts which are wanting in finish; and he will thus be able to take out the loose threads that spoil the fabric of his argument.

Thus does the discipline of the paragraph act as a check upon loose habits of thought; because, where every topic is clearly separated out from all the rest, we may more readily perceive when our view of a topic is incomplete, and may cease to make our essay a mass of undigested ideas.

Paragraph-types. Let us now examine a few leading types of paragraph, in order to observe (1) the manner of introducing a paragraph-subject, and (2) the correct process of its development.

(i) Introductory Paragraph. The paragraph of simplest structure is that which serves merely to break ground in a new subject. This *Introductory* Paragraph states a topic, and leaves it for future consideration; or it draws up a series of topics, and lays down the general plan of an essay.

"It is very hard for the mind to disengage itself from a subject in which it has been long employed. The thoughts will be rising of themselves from time to time, though we give them no encouragement; as the tossings and fluctuations of the sea continue several hours after the winds are laid." [*Spectator*, No. 63.]

"As a single man, I have spent a good deal of my time in noting down the infirmities of Married People, to console myself for those superior pleasures which they tell me I have lost by remaining as I am." ["A Bachelor's Complaint", *Essays of Elia.*]

It is important that the Introductory Paragraph should be as *allusive* and as *picturesque* as possible:

"Having already given my reader an account of several extraordinary clubs, both ancient and modern, I did not design to have troubled him with any more narratives of this nature; but I have lately received information of a club which I can call neither ancient nor modern, that I dare say will be no less surprising to my reader than it was to myself; for which reason I shall communicate it to the public as one of the greatest curiosities in its kind." [*Spectator*, No. 72.]

An allusive statement, arousing the interest of the reader.

Do not start too abruptly ("The subject of my essay is . . ."); but hold a little aloof, and insinuate the subject by means of a general statement descending to particulars, or by an illustration.

"I have observed that a reader seldom peruses a book with pleasure, till he knows whether the writer of it be a black or a fair man, of a mild or choleric disposition, married or a bachelor, with other particulars of the like nature that conduce very much to the right understanding of an author. To gratify this curiosity, which is so natural to a reader, I design this paper and my next as prefatory discourses to my following writings, and shall give some account in them of the several persons that are engaged in this work. As the chief trouble of compiling, digesting, and correcting will fall to my share, I must do myself the justice to open the work with my own history." [*Spectator*, No. 1.]

> A general statement, descending to a particular.
>
> [Remark the sentence-glide: "to gratify this curiosity".]

"Lucian in one of his Dialogues introduces a philosopher chiding his friend for his being a lover of dancing and a frequenter of balls. The other undertakes the defence of his favourite diversion, which he says was at first invented by the Goddess Rhea . . ." [*Spectator*, No. 67.]

> Illustration.

(ii) Intermediate Paragraph. Equally simple in structure is the paragraph that intervenes between two different topics, and serves to make the passage clear from one to the other. This *Intermediate* Paragraph (1) may set the two topics side by side as two co-ordinate propositions; or (2), a more common practice, may indicate the previous topic in a subordinate clause, and introduce the new topic as a principal sentence.

"In short every man here pretends to be a politician; even the fair sex are sometimes found to mix the severity of national altercation with the blandishments of love, and often become conquerors by more weapons of destruction than their eyes." [*Citizen of the World*, Letter iv.]

> Transition from "Liberty" to "Politics" — co-ordinate propositions.

> Previous topic: "it is that they [married couples] are too loving".

"Not too loving neither: that does not explain my meaning. Besides, why should that offend me? The very act of separating themselves from the rest of the world, to have the fuller enjoyment of each other's society, implies that they prefer one another to all the world." ["A Bachelor's Complaint", *Essays of Elia*.]

> Transition by co-ordinate statements to the next topic; which the reader will find introduced by an emphatic *But*, in the beginning of the following paragraph:
> "But what I complain of is that they carry this preference so undisguisedly".

"I could forgive their jealousy, and dispense with toying with their brats, if it gives them any pain; but I think it unreasonable to be called upon to *love* them, where I see no occasion—to love a whole family, perhaps, eight, nine or ten indiscriminately—to love all the pretty dears, because children are so engaging." [*Ib.*]

> Transition from "jealousy of young parents" to the "obligation of loving young children" — co-ordinate statements.

"Having given this short account of the institution and continuation of the Everlasting Club, I should here endeavour to say something of the manners and characters of its several members, which I shall do according to the best lights I have received in this matter." [*Spectator*, No. 72.]

> Subordinate phrase and principal sentence.

"It is observed by Cicero, that men of the greatest and most shining parts are the most actuated by ambition; and, if we look into the two sexes, I believe we shall find this principle of action stronger in women than in men." [*Spectator*, No. 73.]

> Transition from "ambition" to "ambitious women".

"*Behold me, then, in London,* gazing at the strangers, and they at me. It seems they find somewhat absurd in my figure; and, had I never been from home, it is possible I might find an infinite fund of ridicule in theirs: but by long travelling *I am taught to laugh at folly alone and to find nothing truly ridiculous but villainy and vice.*"

Transition from a paragraph of description to one of moral reflection.

(iii) Descriptive Paragraph. In the *Descriptive* Paragraph[1], the subject is (1) explicitly stated in the opening or (2) inferred from the whole. In the latter case it is essential that one definite central topic be implicit, *i.e.* clear to the writer's mind. The writer should take care, in both cases, that the details of the description follow a particular order, that the transitions be easy, and the circumstances of time and place, well-grouped.

"*The bearer* of this is my friend; therefore let him be yours. *He* is a native of Honan in China, and one who did me signal services, when he was a mandarin, and I a factor at *Canton.* By frequently conversing with the English *there*, he has learnt the language, though entirely a stranger to their manners and *customs.* I am told he is a *philosopher*; I am sure he is an honest man. . . ." [*Citizen of the World*, Letter i.]

Remark the easy transitions: *Bearer—he—Canton —there—ignorance of customs—but a philosopher.*

"Thus I live in the world rather as a *spectator* of mankind than as one of the species. . . . In short, I have acted in all the parts of my life as a *looker-on*, which is the character I intend to preserve in this paper." [*Spectator*, No. 1.]

The subject about which descriptive details are given is stated both at the beginning and end.

[1] Under the general title of *Descriptive Paragraph*, I include also the *Narrative Paragraph.*

" He was a (1) *very silent man* by custom. All day he (2) *hung round* the cove, or upon the cliffs with a brass telescope; all evening he (1a) *sat in a corner of the parlour* next the fire, and drank rum and water very strong. Mostly he (1b) *would not speak* when spoken to; only look up sudden and fierce, and blow through his nose like a foghorn; and we and the people who came about our house soon learnt to let him be. (2a) Every day, *when he came back from his stroll*, he would ask if any seafaring men had gone by along the road. At first we thought it was the want of company of his own kind that made him ask this question; but at last we began to see (3) *he was desirous to avoid them.* (3a) When a seaman put up at the "Admiral Benbow" (as now and then some did, making by the coast road for Bristol), he would look in at him through the curtained door before he entered the parlour; and he was always sure to be as silent as a mouse — when any such was present. (4) *For me*, at least, there was *no secret about the matter*; for I was in a way a sharer in his alarms. (4a) He had taken me aside one day, and promised me a silver fourpenny on the first of every month, if I would only keep my 'weather-eye open for a seafaring man with one leg', and let him know the moment he appeared. Often enough, when the first of the month came round, and I applied to him for my wage, he would only blow through his nose at me — and stare me down; but, before the week was out, he was sure to think better of it, bring me my fourpenny piece, and repeat his orders to look out for 'the seafaring man with one leg'."

" The *appearance of the island* when I came on deck next morning was altogether changed. Although the breeze had now utterly failed, we had made a great deal of way during the night, and were now lying becalmed about half a mile to the south-east of the low eastern

Remark how, in the development of the leading topic "he was a silent man", easy transitions are made in the narrative.

(1) *silence* — transition to (2) *strolling on the cliff.*

(1a) and (1b) particularization of silent habit.

(2a) reversion to strolling habit, and easy transition to (3) *his desire to avoid seafaring men.*

(3a) illustration of this fear.

(4) *did not keep his fear secret from Jim.*

(4a) particularization and climax.

Subject for description.

Reason for "change".

Orderly arrangement of striking particulars.

coast. (*a*) *Grey-coloured woods* covered a large part of the *surface*. (*b*) *This even tint* was indeed *broken up* by streaks of yellow sandbreak in the lower lands, and by many tall trees of the pine family, out-topping the others, some singly, some in clumps ; but the general colouring was uniform and sad. (*c*) *The hills* ran up clear above the vegetation in spires of naked rock. All were strangely shaped, and (*d*) *the Spy-glass*, which was by three or four hundred feet the tallest on the island, was likewise the strangest in configuration, running up sheer from almost every side, and then suddenly cut off at the top like a pedestal to put a statue on."	(*a*) grey woods on surface. (*b*) uniformity broken. (*c*) hills rising above surface. (*d*) natural glide to the 'hill' on which attention is to be concentrated—"the Spy-glass".

In a paragraph which carries a number of descriptive particulars that bear continually on the same subject, it is often expedient to keep the structure of the sentences the same (*Balance of Sentences*). This device makes the subject to be described prominent throughout, and effectively groups the co-related particulars.

"A FORWARD BOLD MAN

(A) "Is a lusty fellow in a crowd, that's beholding more to his elbow than his legs, for he does not go, but thrusts well. HE is a good shuffler in the world, wherein he is so oft putting forth, that at length he puts on. HE can do something, but dare do much more, and is like a desperate soldier, who will assault anything where he is sure not to enter. (B) HE is not so well opinion'd of himself, as industrious to make other; and thinks no vice so prejudicial as blushing. HE is still citing for himself, that a candle should not be hid under a bushel, and for his part, he will be sure not to hide his, though his candle be but a snuff or rush candle. (C) These few good parts he has, he is no niggard in displaying,	Remark: (i) that the subject of description takes the same position in every sentence. (ii) that the sentences are parallel in structure ; the first three (A) contain each two subordinate clauses : then follow two sentences (B) consisting each of two co-ordinate parts ; while each of the two co-ordinate parts contains a subordinate clause. (C) The balance is then

and is like some needy flaunting Gold-smith, nothing in the inner room, but all on the cupboard. If he be a scholar, he has commonly stept into the Pulpit before a degree; yet into that too, before he deserv'd it. (D) HE never defers St. Mary's beyond his regency, and his next sermon is at Paul's Cross, and that printed. HE loves public things alife: and for any solemn entertainment he will find a mouth, find a speech who will. HE is greedy of great acquaintance and many, and thinks it no small advancement to rise to be known, *etc.*" [EARLE, *Micro-cosmographie* (Arber), p. 47.]

relieved, during two sentences. (D) After this the structure again grows parallel, the subject of description having front-position as before; and each sentence consisting of two co-ordinate parts.

(iv) Paragraph of Summary. The *Paragraph of Summary* is short and simple, and subject to no definite laws of progression. The writer must, however, be careful to confine himself severely to the material he has already employed, and *to avoid indication of any fresh opening.*

"When men are thus knit together by love of society, not a spirit of faction, and do not meet to censure or annoy those that are absent, but to enjoy one another; when they are thus combined for their own improvement, or for the good of others, or at least to relax themselves from the business of the day by an inno-cent and cheerful conversation, there may be something very useful in these little institutions and establishments." [*Spec-tator*, No. 9.]

Paragraph conclud-ing the essay on "Clubs".

(v) Predicative Paragraph. This is the paragraph of the kind most common in the ordinary theme or essay. The writer proposes a definite topic and variously amplifies it with predicative matter. The different means of *amplifying* a paragraph-topic being almost incapable of exhaustion, I intend here

G

merely to examine some dominant types of the predicative order of paragraph, for the purpose of indicating to the beginner in prose a method of inquiry he should pursue for himself.

Place of the Paragraph-Topic. The question of first regard is the *place* of the paragraph-topic; for, in the predicative paragraph, that topic must be explicitly stated somewhere. The rule may be formulated at once (and it is a rule admitting of few exceptions): the paragraph-topic should stand prominently in front of its amplification, just as in the sentence the logical subject precedes all predicative matter.

"Man is said to be a *sociable animal*. . . ." [*Spectator*, No. 9.]

"Going yesterday to dine with an old acquaintance, I had the misfortune to find his whole *family very much dejected*." [*Spectator*, No. 7.]

Exceptions. (1) Suspension of the topic of a paragraph is by no means so common as suspension of the subject of a sentence. It does, however, happen sometimes that the paragraph-subject appears as a conclusion drawn from preceding detail.

"When I had just quitted my native country, and crossed the Chinese wall, I fancied every deviation from the customs and manners of China was a departing from nature. I smiled at the blue lips and red foreheads of the Tonguese; and could hardly contain when I saw the Daures dress their heads with horns; the Ostiacs powdered with red earth, and the Calmuck beauties tricked out in all the finery of sheepskin, appeared highly ridiculous. But I soon perceived that the ridicule lay not in them, but in me;   **Detail.**

that I falsely condemned others for absur- | Conclusion.
dity, because they happened to differ
from a standard orginally founded in
prejudice or partiality." [*Citizen of the
World*, Letter iii.]

(2) Or again, the real paragraph-topic may be introduced at the close in opposition to the apparent topic of the paragraph.

" The display of superior knowledge or
riches may be made sufficiently morti-
fying; but these admit of a palliative.
The knowledge which is brought out to | Apparent topic.
insult me may accidentally improve me;
and in the rich man's houses and pictures,
his parks and gardens, I have a tempo-
rary usufruct at least. But the display | Real topic.
of married happiness has none of these
palliatives; it is throughout pure, unre-
compensed, unqualified insult." [*Essays
of Elia*, " A Bachelor's Complaint ".

Professor Minto said of Macaulay: " One of his greatest arts of suspense is to occupy the first sentence of the paragraph with circumstances leading us to expect the opposite of what is really the main statement ".

This introduction of the paragraph-topic by the device of contrast is illustrated in the following, where the writer begins with a statement that apparently refers to another subject, and then with an emphatic *but* forces in the true paragraph-topic.

" In the old drama there had been
much that was reprehensible. BUT, who- | An emphatic " but "
ever compares even the least decorous | introduces the true
plays of Fletcher with those contained | paragraph-topic.
in the volume before us, will see how
much the profligacy, which follows a

period of overstrained austerity, goes beyond the profligacy, which precedes such a period." [MACAULAY on the "Restoration Dramatists."]

"I know there is a proverb, 'Love me, love my dog'; that is not always so very practicable, particularly if the dog be set upon you to tease you or snap at you in sport. But a dog, or a lesser thing—any inanimate substance, as a keepsake, a watch, or a ring, a tree, or the place where we last parted when my friend went away upon a long absence—I can make shift to love, because I love him, and anything that reminds me of him; provided it be in its nature indifferent, and apt to receive whatever hue fancy can give it. But children have a real character and an essential being of themselves: they are amiable or unamiable *per se*; I must love or hate them as I see cause for either in their qualities." [*Essays of Elia*, "A Bachelor's Complaint."]

Here the pseudo-topic is amplified, to make the contrast more effective.

(3) A further exception to the general rule is to be found in the fact that the paragraph-topic may not appear at all. This happens only when the Predicative Paragraph has been immediately preceded by a paragraph of an Introductory kind which proposes the topic to be amplified; the predicative paragraph is then concerned only with amplification. The paragraph immediately succeeding the one quoted above (under exception (1)) is a particularization of the conclusion already arrived at—"that standards of taste are founded in prejudice or partiality". This conclusion it leads forward to another conclusion of a more general kind. The paragraph-topic is not explicitly stated.

" I find no pleasure, therefore, in taxing the English with departing from nature in their external appearance, which is all I yet know of their character : it is possible they only endeavour to improve her simple plan, since every extravagance in dress proceeds from a desire of becoming more beautiful than nature made us ; and this is so harmless a vanity, that I not only pardon, but approve it. A desire to be more excellent than others is what actually makes us so; and, as thousands find a livelihood in society by such appetites, none but the ignorant inveigh against them." [*Citizen of the World*, Letter iii.]

Particularization of previous proposition.

A more general conclusion.

The Paragraph-Glide. It is necessary not only that the topic of the paragraph should be moved in the first sentence, but also that it should be at the same time effectively linked to the leading topic of the preceding paragraph. Sometimes the sequence is so close, that no deliberate effort of connection is required. When deliberate connection is necessary, it must be made incidental to the proposition of the new paragraph-topic.

(i) Connection given by a *leading word or phrase* :

" You are not insensible what numberless (1) *trades*, even among the Chinese, subsist by the (2) *harmless pride* of each other ". [*Citizen of the World*, Letter iii.]

(1) New topic.
(2) Old topic : "the harmless vanity of the English ".

" In the formation of character almost everything depends upon (1) *these two influences*, whether the tendency of them be (2) *good or bad*."

(1) old topic.

(2) new topic.

" This (1) *grand scene of business* gave me an infinite variety of solid and substantial (2) *entertainments*." [*Spectator*, No. 69.]

(1) old topic.

(2) new topic.

(1) " *For these reasons*, there are no more useful members in a commonwealth than (2) *merchants*." [*Spectator*, No. 69.]	(1) old topic.
	(2) new topic.
"Nature seems to have taken a particular care to disseminate her blessings among the different regions of the world, *with an eye to this mutual intercourse and traffic among mankind*." [*Spectator*, No. 69.]	The reference to the old topic should, if possible, come first. It would have been better therefore: "With an eye to this mutual intercourse and traffic among mankind, nature seems, &c.".

(ii) The new topic explicitly opposed or cumulated to the old:

"But, as this (1) *passion for admiration*, when it works according to reason, improves the beautiful part of our species in everything that is laudable; so nothing is more destructive to them, when it is (2) *governed by vanity and folly* ". [*Spectator*, No. 73.]	(1) old topic. (2) new topic.
(1) " *Those whom I have now been describing* affect the gravity of the lion; (2) *those I am going to describe* more resemble the pert vivacity of smaller animals." [*Citizen of the World*, Letter iii.]	(1) old topic. (2) new topic.
" But, notwithstanding (1) *man's essential perfection* is but very little, his (2) *comparative perfection* may be very considerable." [*Spectator*, No. 73.]	(1) old topic. (2) new topic.

In the following, the new topics are cumulated, with or without mention of the old:

" But this is not the worst ".	
" Then there is the exaggerating way, or the way of irony."	
" The poet before us has not only (1) *found out an hero in his own country*, but raises the reputation of it by (2) *several beautiful incidents*." [*Spectator*, No. 70.]	(1) old topic. (2) new topic.
" But what surprises me more than all the rest is what I have just now been credibly informed of by one of this country." [*Citizen of the World*, Letter iii.]	

(iii) The old topic grammatically subordinated to the new:

"Yet, (1) *uncivil as nature has been*, they seem resolved to (2) *outdo her in kindness*". [*Citizen of the World*, Letter iii.]	(1) old topic. (2) new topic.
"What they want however, in (1) *gaiety*, they make up in (2) *politeness*." [*Citizen of the World*, Letter iv.]	(1) old topic. (2) new topic.
"But, lest (1) *this fine description* should be excepted against as the creation of that great master, Mr. Dryden, and not an account of what has really ever happened in the world, I shall give you verbatim the (2) *epistle of an enamoured footman in the country to his mistress*." [*Spectator*, No. 7.]	(1) old topic. (2) new topic.
"Yet, when I consider what sort of a creature the (1) *fine lady* is, (2) *to whom he is supposed to pay his addresses*, it is not strange to find him thus equipped in order to please."	(1) new topic. (2) old topic.

The First Sentence. Care must be had—

(1) That the topic proposed in the first sentence be the real topic of the paragraph.

(2) That the real paragraph-topic be not obscured.

(1) In the following, as may be gathered from the first sentence of the *Amplification*, the subject proposed is not the real topic of the paragraph.

"We find it needful in the great *events* of life, and in its smallest circumstances. To the king upon his throne, as well as to his meanest subject, common-sense is . . ."	The topic clearly is not "events" but "persons".
"To make *a fine gentleman*, several trades are required, but chiefly a barber. You have undoubtedly heard of the Jewish champion, whose strength lay in his hair; one would think that the Eng-	The topic of the paragraph proves to be not "the making of a fine gentleman", but "the making of a wise

lish were for placing all wisdom there: man ".   For   " fine to appear wise, nothing more is requisite gentleman " therefore here than for a man to borrow hair from write " wise man ". the heads of all his neighbours, and clap it like a bush on his own. . . ." [*Citizen of the World*, Letter iii.]

(2) In the following, two subjects seemed to be proposed; the " rareness of common-sense " proved to be the real paragraph-topic. The first sentence, by giving a wrong lead, temporarily diverts from the true topic.

	STRUCTURE CORRECT.
Common-sense we may define for our present purpose as *sound judgement.* It is a quality *more rarely met with* than its name implies.	Common-sense, which for our present purpose we may define as sound judgement, is a quality *more rarely met with* than its name implies.

In the following (*Citizen of the World*, Letter iv.), Goldsmith comes too late to his paragraph-topic. The topic, it will be found, requires to be made prominent by subordinating some matter, and by omitting other matter that tends to obscure it.

" The English seem as silent as the Japanese, yet *vainer* than the inhabitants of Siam."

This suggests for a paragraph-topic " English vanity ". However, in the next sentence,

" Upon my arrival I attributed that reserve to modesty, which I now find has its origin in *pride*",

we arrive at what proves to be the real paragraph-topic, " English pride ". The diverting clause referring to " vanity " should therefore be omitted, and that referring to " silence " subordinated, thus:

" The English seem as silent as the Japanese; this reserve, which upon my arrival I attributed to modesty, I now find has its origin in *pride* ".

We have now stated the rules which it is necessary to observe in regard to the *subject* of the paragraph (*i.e.* the proposition of the paragraph-topic). Remark especially:

(*a*) The necessity for a paragraph-glide.

(*b*) That the topic proposed in the *Subject* of the paragraph be the real topic.

(*c*) That the *subject* of the paragraph may sometimes be suspended.

(*d*) That the topic may be stated illustratively, or brought in with a " but".

General Scheme of the Predicative Paragraph. It will be found that the Predicative Paragraph conforms in general to the following scheme:

A. (1) SUBJECT of the paragraph.

(2) The COPULA or LINK between Subject and Predicate.

B. PREDICATE of the paragraph.

C. The PARAGRAPH-CLOSE.

The *Subject* and the *Predicate* are of course constant parts of the structure of the Predicative Paragraph; the *Copula* and *Paragraph-close* are not always present.

Frequently, however, the Subject requires *explanation* (iteration, definition, or the like) before it is confirmed; and further, the paragraph may be rounded off by the *application* of the predicative matter to the Subject; as in the following example:

"One would think that the larger the company is, in which we are engaged, the greater variety of thoughts and subjects would be started in discourse; but, instead of this, we find that conversation is never so much straitened and confined as in numerous assemblies. When a multitude meet together upon any subject of discourse, their debates are taken up chiefly with forms and general positions; nay, if we come into a more contracted assembly of men and women, the talk generally runs upon the weather, fashions, news, and the like public topics. In proportion as conversation gets into clubs and knots of friends, it descends into particulars, and grows more free and communicative. But the most open, instructive, and unreserved discourse is that which passes between two persons who are familiar and intimate friends. On these occasions a man gives a loose to every passion and every thought that is uppermost, discovers his most retired opinions of persons and things, tries the beauty and strength of his sentiments, and exposes his whole soul to the examination of his friend." [*Spectator*, No. 68.]

A. (1) SUBJECT stated allusively.

(2) COPULA or LINK —Explanation of subject.

B. PREDICATE—the Predicative Matter here consists in *particulars* concerning the subject.

C. PARAGRAPH-CLOSE, which is here an *application* of the Predicative matter.

The Copula or Link. The structure of the Predicative Paragraph may be seriously impaired by the omission of a necessary *Copula* between the Subject and Predicate. Especially is this the case when the Copula takes the form of an *Explanation* of the Subject-matter. By the omission of the *Explanation* (a common fault in the student's essay), the connection between the Subject and Predicate of the paragraph, is frequently lost:

"There is a certain sense in which a man or woman having common-sense is less selfish than one who is without it [*explanation here omitted*]. We are

The SUBJECT needs a link:
For common-sense is in one of its aspects a sense

all familiar with the people who seem entirely forgetful of the ordinary responsibilities of life; they are utterly regardless of the great amount of trouble and anxiety that they cause to others. We think them selfish people, but *this thoughtless selfishness might be greatly diminished by a use of common-sense.*"

of our common responsibilities. (EXPLANATION.)

Then follow correctly the ILLUSTRATIVE PARTICULARS.

It would be better to refer the last sentence more explicitly to the paragraph-topic, thus supplying an APPLICATION:

this thoughtless selfishness *is in reality a defect of common-sense.* (APPLICATION.)

"The advantage of common-sense does not seem always to have been sufficiently recognized. We frequently hear ability praised, and justly so, but [*explanation here omitted*] without common-sense its usefulness is greatly marred."

The *explanation* is here not sufficiently definite: the thought is elliptical. Insert:

but *the quality of common-sense is not so frequently or so justly recognized, yet* without common-sense . . .

"Pride seems the source not only of their national vices, but of their national virtues also [*explanation here omitted*]. An Englishman despises those nations who, that *one* may be free, are all content to be slaves; who first lift a *tyrant* into terror, and then shrink under his power as if delegated from Heaven, &c." [*Citizen of World*, Letter iv.]

SUBJECT.

EXPLANATION (omitted here):

"*An Englishman is taught to love his king as his friend, but to acknowledge no other master which himself has contributed to enact.* He despises . . .*"

The Predicative Matter. In order to assist further inquiry into the structure of the Predicative Paragraph, let us now examine some of the forms that the Amplification, or the *Predicative Matter*, of the paragraph may take.

(i) Particularization. The Predicative Matter of the paragraph may, in the first place, take the form of a *Particularization*, which confirms the

Subject of the paragraph, as in the following example:

"Nature seems to have taken a particular care to disseminate her blessings among the different regions of the world, with an eye to this mutual intercourse and traffic among mankind; that the natives of the several parts of the globe might have a kind of dependence upon one another, and be united together by their common interest. Almost every degree produces something peculiar to it. The food often grows in one country, and the sauce in another. The fruits of Portugal are corrected by the products of Barbados; the infusion of a China plant sweetened with the pith of an Indian cane. The Philippic Islands give a flavour to our European bowls. The single dress of a woman of quality is often the product of a hundred climates. The muff and the fan . . . etc." [*Spectator*, No. 69.]

A. SUBJECT.

B. PREDICATIVE MATTER—Illustrative Particulars.

The *Particulars* in this type of paragraph may be

(1) an illustration of the general proposition, or

(2) an application of some general principle stated as the proposition.

" Yet, uncivil as nature has been, they seem resolved to outdo her in unkindness. They use white powder, blue powder, and black powder for their hair, and a red powder for the face on some particular occasions. They like to have the face of various colours, &c." [*Citizen of World*, Letter iii.]

SUBJECT — general proposition.
PARTICULARS, merely illustrative.

"The inevitable consequence of poverty is dependence. Dryden had probably no recourse in his exigencies but to his booksellers. The particular character of Tonson, &c." [Johnson, *Life of Dryden*.]

SUBJECT—a general principle.
PARTICULAR APPLICATION of same to the case of Dryden.

(ii) **Generalization.** We may, on the other hand, proceed from the particular to the general. The Predicative Matter then takes the form of a *Generalization* of that particular instance, which is stated as the subject of the paragraph. This type of paragraph is very common in the Essay, and consequently a favourite form with Charles Lamb. Its structure is:

A. SUBJECT.—Proposition of a particular instance.

B. PREDICATE.—Confirmation by generalization: aided frequently by an illustration.
   The particular leads to general.

C. PARAGRAPH-CLOSE.—Application.
   The general is led back to the particular.

"But what I complain of is, that they carry this preference so undisguisedly, they perk it up in the faces of us single people so shamelessly, you cannot be in their company a moment without being made to feel by some indirect hint or open avowal, that *you* are not the object of this preference. Now there are some things which give no offence, while implied or taken for granted merely; but expressed, there is much offence in them. If a man were to accost the first homely-featured or plain-dressed young woman of his acquaintance, and tell her bluntly that she was not handsome or rich enough for him, and he could not marry her, he would deserve to be kicked for his ill-manners; yet no less is implied in the fact that, having access and opportunity of putting the question to her, he has never yet thought fit to do it. The young woman understands this as clearly as if it were put into words; but no reasonable young woman would think of making

A. SUBJECT — particular.

B. PREDICATE—Confirmation by—
(*a*) a generalization,

and (*b*) an example.

this a ground of quarrel. Just as little
right have a married couple to tell me
by speeches, and looks that are scarce less
plain than speeches, that I am not the
happy man — the lady's choice. It is
enough that I know that I am not; I do
not want this perpetual reminding." [*Essays of Elia*, " A Bachelor's Complaint."]

C. PARAGRAPH-CLOSE—Application.

(iii) **Reason.** The Subject of the paragraph may be confirmed also by a *Reason*, which must be always followed by an *Application*.

"Certain I am, O thou instructor of my youth, that, without philosophers, without some few virtuous men, who seem to be of a different nature from the rest of mankind, without such as these, the worship of a wicked divinity would surely be established over every part of the earth. Fear guides more to their duty than gratitude: for one man, who is virtuous from the love of virtue, from the obligation, which he thinks he lies under to the Giver of all, there are ten thousand, who are good only from their apprehensions of punishment. Could these last be persuaded, as the Epicureans were, that heaven had no thunders in store for the villain, they would no longer continue to acknowledge subordination, or thank that Being who gave them existence." (*Citizen of the World*, Lett. x.)

A. SUBJECT.

B. PREDICATE.
Reason.

C. APPLICATION.

(iv) **Particularization and Illustration.** A more fully-developed form of the predicative matter is indicated in the following scheme:

Among the several qualifications of a good friend, this wise man has very justly singled out constancy and faithfulness as the principal: to these, others have added virtue, knowledge, discretion, equality in age and fortune, and, as Cicero calls it, *morum comitas*, a pleasantness of

A. SUBJECT.

temper. If I were to give my opinion upon such an exhausted subject, I should join to these other qualifications a certain equability or evenness of behaviour: a man often contracts a friendship with one whom perhaps he does not find out till after a year's conversation; when on a sudden some latent ill-humour breaks out upon him, which he never discovered or suspected at his first entering into an intimacy with him. There are several persons who in some certain periods of their lives are inexpressibly agreeable, and in others as odious and detestable. Martial has given us a very pretty picture of one of this species in the following epigram:

. . . .

It is very unlucky for a man to be entangled in a friendship with one who by these changes and vicissitudes of humour is sometimes amiable and sometimes odious: and, as most men are at some times in an admirable frame and disposition of mind, it should be one of the greatest tasks of wisdom to keep ourselves well when we are so, and never to go out of that which is the agreeable part of our character. [*Spectator*, No. 68.]

B. PREDICATE—
(1) Particularization by Detail.

(2) Illustration.

C. PARAGRAPH - CLOSE — Conclusions drawn.

A more fully-developed Scheme of a Predicative Paragraph. From the above examples it will be seen that the good paragraph invariably adapts itself to some definite scheme of development. It would be futile in the writer to attempt to work to any definite scheme; but he may keep some definite scheme before his mind's eye, and, when he arrives at the second act of composition—the critical act—he may correct his work by the scheme. Moreover, no observation of the writing of others can be really critical (that is really fruitful) unless the reader knows this accidence of style; knowing himself the laws and liberties of writing, he may then to some useful purpose observe the actual practice of writers. He will find that, only by following closely, or by afterwards squaring his work to some definite structural scheme, is it possible to avoid digression and superfluity, and to secure regularity of growth. The various parts of the paragraph—Particularization, Reason, Illustration—may occur separately, or they may, in the fullest form, be combined. They should, in any case, be introduced in an orderly manner; and their bearing upon the paragraph-topic should be assured. In the following scheme of a Predicative Paragraph there may be seen at what periods in the growth of the paragraph the different stages in its development are reached.

THE PREDICATIVE PARAGRAPH.

A. (1) Subject of the Paragraph.

Proposition of the Paragraph-topic.
Note (*a*) the necessity for a paragraph-glide;
(*b*) that the topic proposed be the *real topic*;
(*c*) that it may sometimes be suspended, even till the close;
(*d*) that it may be stated illustratively, or brought in with a 'but'.

(2) The Copula, or Link between Subject and Predicate.

(i) Explanation of the Paragraph-subject.
Notice when it is possible to omit the explanation.
(ii) Iteration.
In cases where it is advisable to repeat for emphasis' sake the Paragraph-subject, throw, by the use of a synonymous expression, a fresh light on the thought.

B. PREDICATE OF THE PARAGRAPH.
- (i) GENERALIZATION.
- (ii) PARTICULARIZATION.
- (iii) ILLUSTRATIVE DETAIL.
- (iv) ILLUSTRATIVE INSTANCES, or COMPARISONS.

C. THE PARAGRAPH-CLOSE.
- (i) APPLICATION of the particular to the general, or of the general to the particular.
- (ii) A SUMMARY, or a distinct AFFIRMATION of the Paragraph-subject.
- (iii) The CONCLUSIONS drawn from the Paragraph-subject.

MISCELLANEOUS EXAMPLES OF PARAGRAPH-STRUCTURE.

THE PARAGRAPH OF SUMMARY.

"A great deal must be allowed to Pope for the age in which he lived, and not a little, I think, for the influence of Swift. In his own province he still stands unapproachably alone. If to be the greatest satirist of individual men, rather than of human nature, if to be the highest expression which the life of the court and the ball-room has ever found in verse, if to have added more phrases to our language than any other but Shakespeare, if to have charmed four generations make a man a great poet,—then he is one. He was the chief founder of an artificial style of writing, which in his hands was living and powerful, because he used it to express artificial modes of thinking and an artificial state of society. Measured by any high standard of imagination, he will be found wanting; tried by any test of wit, he is unrivalled." [J. RUSSELL LOWELL, *Essay on Pope*.]

Remark that in this PARAGRAPH OF SUMMARY, the topics are arranged with a view to *climax*, while *no digression* is caused by amplifying any topic.

(i) Influences on Pope.

(ii) Pope alone in his own province.

(iii) Pope a poet.

(iv) But the founder of an artificial style.

(v) Wanting in imagination; unrivalled in wit.

THE PARAGRAPH OF DESCRIPTION.

"The troops were exceeding fine, well-accoutred, brave, clean-limbed, stout fellows indeed. Here I saw the cardinal. There was an air of church gravity in his habit, but all the vigour of a general, and the sprightliness of a vast genius in his face. He affected a little stiffness in his behaviour, but managed all his affairs with such clearness, such steadiness, and such application, that it was no wonder he had such success in every undertaking." [DEFOE, *Memoirs of a Cavalier.*]

In this DESCRIPTIVE PARAGRAPH, the first sentence gives a "wrong lead". The subject is not *troops*, but *cardinal*. Omit therefore the first sentence. The description of the *cardinal* is consecutive enough; passing naturally from his "physical" to his "moral" aspect.

"Though fond of many acquaintances, I desire an intimacy only with a few. The Man in Black, whom I have often mentioned, is one whose friendship I could wish to acquire, because he possesses my esteem. His manners, it is true, are tinctured with some strange inconsistencies; and he may be justly termed an humorist in a nation of humorists. Though he is generous even to profusion, he affects to be thought a prodigy of parsimony and prudence; though his conversation be replete with the most sordid and selfish maxims, his heart is dilated with the most unbounded love. I have known him profess himself a man-hater, while his cheek was glowing with compassion; and, while his looks were softened into pity, I have heard him use the language of the most unbounded ill-nature. Some affect humanity and tenderness; others boast of having such dispositions from nature: but he is the only man I ever knew, who seemed ashamed of his natural benevolence. He takes as much pains to hide his feelings, as any hypocrite would, to conceal his indifference; but, on every unguarded moment, the mask drops off, and reveals him to the most superficial observer." [GOLDSMITH, *Citizen of the World*, Letter x.]

The SUBJECT of this DESCRIPTIVE PARAGRAPH is introduced by a *general* observation descending to a *particular*—a very picturesque method.

Remark also how the details of the Description descend also from the general to the particular, i.e. from "strange inconsistencies" to the special eccentricity, which the author wishes to emphasize — his *inverted hypocrisy*.

This eccentricity is amplified by illustrative detail.

The author *applies* the illustration, and throws thereby new light upon the subject.

"The bobolinks build in considerable numbers in a meadow within a quarter of a mile of us. A houseless lane passes through the midst of their camp, and in clear westerly weather, at the right season, one may hear a score of them singing at once. When they are breeding, if I chance to pass, one of the male birds always accompanies me like a constable, flitting from post to post of the rail-fence, with a short note of reproof continually repeated, till I am fairly out of the neighbourhood. Then he will swing away into the air and run down the wind, gurgling music without stint over the unheeding tussocks of meadow-grass and dark clumps of bulrushes that mark his domain." [J. RUSSELL LOWELL, *My Garden Acquaintance*.]

Observe again in this DESCRIPTIVE PARA-GRAPH the continuous descent from the *general* to the *particular*, by the following stages:

(i) The bobolinks' home.

(ii) Their singing heard in the lane that passes through their camp.

(iii) The behaviour of *one* of them during the breeding-season.

A CONSTABLE

"Is a Vice-roy in the street, and no man stands more upon't that he is the King's Officer. His Jurisdiction extends to the next stocks, where he has Commission for the heels only, and sets the rest of the body at liberty. He is a scarecrow to that Ale-house, where he drinks not his morning's draught, and apprehends a Drunkard for not standing in the King's name. Beggars fear him more than the Justice, and as much as the Whip-stock, whom he delivers over to his subordinate Magistrates, the Bridewell-man, and the Beadle. He is a great stickler in the tumults of double Jugs, and ventures his head by his Place, which is broke many times to keep whole the peace. He is never so much in his Majesty as in his Night-watch, where he sits in his Chair of State, a Shop-stall, and invíron'd with a guard of Halberts, examines all passengers. He is a very careful man in his Office, but if he stays up after Midnight, you shall take him napping." [EARLE, *Micro-cosmographie*.]

The DESCRIPTION here takes a categorical form : item, a vice-roy; item, his jurisdiction; item, his treatment of ale-houses, and so forth.

A *Parallelism* or *Balance* of Structure is here essential, in order to keep that subject prominent, to which the details refer.

It is also necessary in such a paragraph (*a*) to group the details according to their relative importance, and their relation to each other, and (*b*) to aim at a climax in the last sentence—if possible, as in the present example, an epigrammatic climax.

"The standing figure was the first to speak. He was a grey-haired, broad-

In this DESCRIPTIVE PARAGRAPH, the sub-

shouldered man, of the type which, in Tuscan phrase, is moulded with the fist and polished with the pickaxe; but the self-important gravity which had written itself out in the deep lines about his brow and mouth, seemed intended to correct any contemptuous inferences from the hasty workmanship which nature had bestowed on his exterior. He had deposited a large well-filled bag, made of skins, on the pavement: and before him hung a pedlar's basket, garnished partly with small woman's-ware, such as thread and pins; and partly with fragments of glass, which had probably been taken in exchange for those commodities." [GEORGE ELIOT, *Romola*.]

ject, *the standing figure*, is explicitly stated in the opening sentence.

Observe:

(*a*) that the two sentences in the description are parallel in structure, each beginning with a pronoun of explicit reference *he*.

(*b*) that the first sentence contains details of personal appearance only; and the second details of action and position.

"(I) In a deep curve of the mountains lay *a breadth of green land*, curtained by gentle tree-shadowed *slopes* leaning towards the rocky heights. Up *these slopes* might be seen here and there, gleaming between the tree-tops, a *pathway* leading to a little irregular mass of *building* that seemed to have clambered in a hasty way up the mountain-side, and taken a difficult stand there for the sake of showing *the tall belfry* as a sight of beauty to the scattered and clustered houses of the village below. (2) The rays of the newly-risen sun fell obliquely on the westward horn of this crescent-shaped nook: all else lay in dewy shadow. (3) No sound came across the stillness; the very waters seemed to have curved themselves there for rest." [GEORGE ELIOT, *Romola*.]

This is a DESCRIPTIVE PARAGRAPH of a different kind: no subject is explicitly stated in the opening. Remark the *grouping* of the paragraph—

(1) THE LANDSCAPE —the order here corresponds to the order of vision. Moreover, each sentence gives the cue for the next:

(*a*) *a breadth of green land* with *slopes*;

(*b*) on the *slopes* a *pathway*;

(*c*) the *pathway* leads to a mass of *building* with *belfry* above.

(2) LIGHT AND SHADOW.

(3) SOUND.

THE PREDICATIVE PARAGRAPH.

"The condition of the English mind at the close of the seventeenth century was such as to make it particularly sensitive to

This is a very simple form of the PREDICATIVE PARAGRAPH:

(A) A SUBJECT.

the magnetism which streamed to it from Paris. The loyalty of everybody, both in politics and religion, had been put out of joint. A generation of materialists, by the natural rebound which inevitably follows over-tension, was to balance the ultra-spiritualism of the Puritans. As always when a political revolution has been wrought by moral agencies, the plunder had fallen mainly to the share of the greedy, selfish, and unscrupulous, whose disgusting cant had given a taint of hypocrisy to piety itself. Religion, from a burning conviction of the soul, had grown to be with both parties a political badge, as little typical of the inward man as the scallop of a pilgrim. Sincerity is impossible, unless it pervade the whole being, and the pretence of it saps the very foundation of character. There seems to have been an universal scepticism, and in its worst form, that is, with an outward conformity in the interest of decorum and order. There was an unbelief that did not believe even in itself." [J. RUSSELL LOWELL, *Essay on Pope*.]

"There are men whose charm is in their entirety. Their words occasionally utter what their looks invariably express. We read their thoughts by the light of their smiles. Not to see and hear these men is not to know them, and criticism without personal knowledge is in their case mutilation. Those who did know them listen in despair to the half-hearted praise and clumsy disparagement of critical strangers, and are apt to exclaim, as did the younger Pitt, when some extraneous person was expressing wonder at the enormous

(B) PARTICULARIZATION OF SUBJECT.

(1) The SUBJECT is *the condition of the English mind at the close of the seventeenth century*. Remark that the clause, "such as to make it particularly sensitive to the magnetism which streamed to it from Paris", is merely connective, intended to associate the present topic with that of another paragraph.

(2) PARTICULARIZATION:
(i) Loyalty out of joint.
(ii) A generation of materialists.
(iii) Want of sincerity.
(iv) Universal scepticism.

In such a paragraph (a) the writer should aim at a climax, by reserving his most striking particular to the close, and (b) he should endeavour to make the passage as easy as possible from one particular to the next.

The present paragraph is worthy of the fullest regard, as being ideal in both these respects.

A. (1) The SUBJECT consists of *one* sentence: *the charm of some men is in their entirety*.

(2) The EXPLANATION consists of *three* sentences: *we must know their looks as well as their words*, thus showing what the writer means by *entirety*.

B. The PREDICATE, beginning at *Those who did know them*, is of the form of an *Illustrative Detail*.

Its application to the Sub-

reputation of Fox, 'Ah! you have never been under the wand of the magician'." [AUGUSTINE BIRRELL, *Essay on Emerson.*]

"The allegory bodies forth the trials which beset the life of man in all conditions and at all times. But Spenser could never have seen in England such a strong and perfect image of the allegory itself—with the wild wanderings of its personages, its daily chances of battle and danger, its hairbreadth escapes, its strange encounters, its prevailing anarchy and violence, its normal absence of order and law—as he had continually and customarily before him in Ireland. 'The curse of God was so great,' writes John Hooker, a contemporary, 'and the land so barren both of man and beast, that whosoever did travel from one end to the other of all Munster, even from Waterford to Limerick, about six score miles, he should not meet man, woman, or child, saving in cities or towns, nor yet see any beast, save foxes, wolves, or other ravening beasts.' It is the desolation through which Spenser's Knights pursue their solitary way, or join company as they can. Indeed, to read the same writer's account, for instance, of Raleigh's adventures with the Irish chieftains, his challenges and *single* combats, his escapes at fords and woods, is like reading bits of the *Faery Queen* in prose. As Spenser chose to write of knight-errantry, his picture of it has doubtless gained in truth and strength by his very practical experience of what such life as he describes must be. The *Faery Queen* might almost be called the epic of the English wars in Ireland under Elizabeth,

ject being very clear, no Paragraph-close is necessary.

A. The SUBJECT is here suspended, being introduced with a "but" in the second sentence. The subject is then stated so precisely that it requires no explanation.

B. The PREDICATE introduces *Illustrative Detail.*

C. The PARAGRAPH-CLOSE is in the form of an *application* of this illustrative detail to the subject. This *application* is then further confirmed by illustration: the likeness of Raleigh's real adventures to incidents in the *Faery Queen.*

This *application* is followed by a distinct *Affirmation* of the Paragraph-subject, namely,

as much as the epic of English virtue and valour at the same period." [DEAN CHURCH, *Spenser*.]

"But I have been led away from my immediate purpose. I did not intend to compare Shakespeare with the ancients, much less to justify his defects by theirs. Shakespeare himself has left us a pregnant satire on dogmatical and categorical æsthetics in the cloud-scene between Hamlet and Polonius, suggesting exquisitely how futile is any attempt at a cast-iron definition of those perpetually metamorphic impressions of the beautiful, whose source is as much in the man who looks as in the thing he sees. In the fine arts a thing is either good in itself or it is nothing. It neither gains nor loses by having it shown that another good thing was also good in itself, any more than a bad thing profits by comparison with another that is worse. The final judgment of the world is intuitive, and is based, not on proof that a work possesses some of the qualities of another whose greatness is acknowledged, but on the immediate feeling that it carries to a high point of perfection certain qualities proper to itself. One does not flatter a fine pear by comparing it to a fine peach, nor learn what a fine peach is by tasting ever so many poor ones. The boy who makes his first bite into one does not need to ask his father if or how or why it is good. Because continuity is a merit in some kinds of writing, shall we refuse ourselves to the authentic charm of Montaigne's want of it? I have heard people complain of French tragedies because they were

that the poem is indeed "the epic of the English wars in Ireland under Elizabeth". This is an ideal last sentence.

The first *two* sentences are of a *connective* kind.

A. (1) The SUBJECT of the paragraph — the futility of always setting up a definite standard to judge by—is stated *illustratively*.

(2) EXPLANATION.—A piece of fine art "is either good in itself, or it is nothing". This EXPLANATION consists of *three* sentences, each becoming more explicit in its reference to the SUBJECT; until in the third we have it definitely set down that "judgment is not based on proof that a work possesses some of the qualities of another whose greatness is acknowledged".

B. The PREDICATE introduces some *illustrative instances*:

(i) We do not judge a pear by a peach, &c.

(ii) We do not condemn Montaigne's *Essays* for their want of "continuity", though this be a merit of many great writings.

so very French. This, though it may not be to some particular tastes, and may from one point of view be a defect, is from another and far higher a distinguished merit. It is their flavour, as direct a tell-tale of the soil whence they draw it as that of French wines is. Suppose we should tax the Elgin marbles with being too Greek? When will people, nay, when will even critics, get over this self-defrauding trick of cheapening the excellence of one thing by that of another, this conclusive style of judgment which consists simply in belonging to the other parish? *As one grows older*, one loses many idols, perhaps comes at last to have none at all, though he may honestly enough uncover in deference to the worshippers before any shrine. But for the seeming loss the compensation is ample. These saints of literature descend from their canopied remoteness to be even more precious as men like ourselves, our companions in field and street, speaking the same tongue, though in many dialects, and owing one creed under the most diverse masks of form." [J. RUSSELL LOWELL, *Shakespeare Once More*.]

"Surely all men are blind and ignorant of truth. Mankind wanders, unknowing his way, from morning till evening. Where shall we turn after happiness; or is it wisest to desist from the pursuit? Like reptiles in a corner of some stupendous palace, we peep from our holes, look about us, wonder at all we see, but are ignorant of the great architect's design. Oh for a revelation of Himself, for a plan of His universal system! Oh for the reasons of our creation; or why were we created to be thus

(iii) We should not condemn French tragedies " because they are so very French ", *i.e.* because they do not conform to our English standard.

C. The PARAGRAPH-CLOSE is in the form of an *application* of these Illustrative Instances to the Paragraph-subject. We must not " cheapen the excellence" of one thing by comparing it with a definite standard, suggested by another.

At the phrase "as one grows older", it will be noticed that Lowell digresses a little from the real topic of the paragraph, and warns us not to enshrine any writer in "canopied remoteness".

A. (1) The SUBJECT: the first three sentences, though rhetorically effective, do not suggest a definite paragraph-topic.
(2) The EXPLANATION might have followed the phrase "to desist from the pursuit?" This should have been a sentence limiting the general notion of the opening sentences to *our partial view of the scheme of Creation, as a cause of unhappiness.*
B. The PREDICATE begins

unhappy! If we are to experience no other felicity but what this life affords, then are we miserable indeed; if we are born only to look about us, repine and die, then has Heaven been guilty of injustice. If this life terminates my existence, I despise the blessings of Providence, and the wisdom of the giver; if this life be my all, let the following epitaph be written on the tomb of Altangi: "BY MY FATHER'S CRIMES I RECEIVED THIS; BY MY OWN CRIMES I BEQUEATH IT TO MY POSTERITY!" [GOLDSMITH, *Citizen of the World*, Letter ix.]

"The question of Hamlet's madness has been much discussed and variously decided. High medical authority has pronounced, as usual, on both sides of the question. But the induction has been drawn from too narrow premises, being based on a mere diagnosis of the *case*, and not on an appreciation of the character in its completeness. We have a case of pretended madness in the Edgar of 'King Lear'; and it is certainly true that that is a charcoal sketch, coarsely outlined, compared with the delicate drawing, the lights, shades, and half-tints of the portraiture in Hamlet. But does this tend to prove that the madness of the latter, because truer to the recorded observation of experts, is real, and meant to be real, as the other to be fictitious? Not in the least, as it appears to me. Hamlet, among all the characters of Shakespeare, is the most eminently a metaphysician and psychologist. He is a close observer, continually analysing his own nature, and that of others, letting fall his little drops of acid irony with an *illustrative image* ("like reptiles in a corner, &c."), and then *generalizes* from it.

C. The PARAGRAPH-CLOSE —a magnificent climax—is in the form of a *Conclusion* drawn from the lines of Pope, to which, throughout the predicate, he is making an implicit reference:

"Let us, since life can little more supply,
Than *just to look about us and to die;*"

A. SUBJECT.—The first two sentences are general and merely introductory to the special Subject, which is introduced by an emphatic *But* in the third sentence.

B. PREDICATE.—The Subject being now clearly proposed, and needing no additional explanation, the writer proceeds immediately to his Predicate or Amplification. This consists of—

(1) *an Illustrative Instance* —the madness of Edgar in "Lear". The bearing of this instance upon the madness of Hamlet leads to

(2) a PARTICULARIZATION of the whole of Hamlet's case:

(a) that he is a psychologist;

(b) a close observer of things;

(c) possessing a fund of irony; this point is further *illustrated* by his treatment of Ophelia and Osrick.

on all who come near him, to make them show what they are made of. Even Ophelia is not too sacred, Osrick not too contemptible for experiment. If such a man assumed madness he would play his part perfectly. If Shakespeare himself, without going mad, could so observe and remember all the abnormal symptoms as to be able to reproduce them in Hamlet, why should it be beyond the power of Hamlet to reproduce them in himself? If you deprive Hamlet of reason, there is no truly tragic motive left. He would be a fit subject for Bedlam, but not for the stage. We might have pathology enough, but no pathos. Ajax first becomes tragic, when he recovers his wits. If Hamlet is irresponsible, the whole play is a chaos. That he is not so might be proved by evidence enough, were it not labour thrown away." [J. RUSSELL LOWELL, *Shakespeare Once More.*]

C. THE PARAGRAPH-CLOSE (beginning at "If such a man assumed madness") consists of—

(1) an *Application* of the Particulars stated in the Predicate;

(2) a *Conclusion* (beginning at "If you deprive Hamlet of reason") as to what would be the effect of this hypothesis upon the character of the play.

CHAPTER IV.

FIGURES OF PROSE.

Every reader should know of what poetical powers the language is capable, and how far these powers may be exercised in prose. Some definite notions of figured speech should therefore precede any course of reading. The mind is thereby opened to receive the effects of prose, to study those effects, and to imitate them in later exercises. When the writer has mastered the *scheme* of figured speech, he is the more ready to perceive and to employ those resemblances and analogies that aid and beautify thought.

Analogy and Similarity. "There was once a lady", says the old author of the *Ancren Riwle*, "who was beset all about with her foes; her land was devastated, and she was poor. Yet a mighty king's love was turned upon her: he sent her his messengers one after another; and he sent her baubles both many and fair, and succour of food, and help from his own forces. She cared nothing: wherefore he came at last himself, and spoke words so sweet that they might raise the dead to life; and wrought many wonders, and revealed his power, and told her of his kingdom, and offered to make her his queen, who was never worthy to be his slave. Then he suffered a shameful death for love of her. This King is Jesus Christ, Son of God, who in this very manner wooed Man's Soul, which the devils had beset. And He, like a noble wooer, after many messengers and gifts, came to prove His love, &c."

In the above passage, the relation of the great king to the distressed princess is identical with the relation of Christ to man's soul. Now when A bears to B the same relation that C bears to D,

i.e. when A : B :: C : D, or when A : B :: C : B,

then between A and C, there is an *analogy*. An analogy is here established by the author of *Ancren Riwle* between the far king (wooing the distressed princess) and Christ (wooing man's soul).

Again, an Elizabethan writer describes the Spanish galleons as "built high like castles". The galleon and the castle have a quality in common—namely, height. In this single respect they are similar, and a *similarity* may be established between them.

(1) There is an *analogy* between two things, when they each bear the same or a similar relation to something else.

(2) There is a *similarity* between things in respect of the quality or qualities that they have in common.

By reason either of similarity or of analogy, things may be declared *alike*.

In order to be *alike* for the purpose of rhetoric, things should, in general, be *essentially* as *unlike* as possible; that is to say, for figurative resemblance there should, in general, be actual difference in kind. The perception of the point or points of contact between them, the more surprises the reader. "The more remote and unlike in themselves any two objects are, the more is the mind impressed and gratified by the perception of some point in which they agree" (Dr. A. SMITH).

A comparison of things *essentially alike*—a tall man and Saul, a strong man and Samson—though a statement of similarity, is a concrete example, and not a rhetorical figure. The following is a concrete example, because the things compared are identical in kind:

"The title is as long as an ordinary preface; the prefatory matter would furnish out an ordinary book; and the book contains as much reading as an ordinary library".

There is this great difference between a concrete example and a rhetorical figure. A concrete example is a weapon of argument; a rhetorical figure—an analogy or a similarity that we adduce by way of metaphor or simile—may explain and illustrate, but it cannot prove. Much false argument has arisen from taking rhetorical resemblances as literal; the fact that the resemblance is *not literal* is the very virtue that commends it to the rhetorician. As soon as ever we strive to establish a literal resemblance, we push beyond the point at which figurative resemblance ends:

"As we commonly feed on beef hungerly at the first, yet seeing the quail more dainty change our diet; so I, though I loved Philautus for his good properties, yet seeing Euphues to excel him, I ought by nature to love him better".	Taking the resemblance as literal, we might argue cannibal tendencies on the lady's part.
"the *long-eared* race of his critics."	With a literal view, we might argue four legs, herbivorous habits, stubbornness, and all other qualities of the ass.

We must, therefore, be careful not to take at the same time a rhetorical and a literal view of a thing; "not to proceed to a comparison of the corresponding terms as they are intrinsically *in themselves*, or in their own nature, but merely as they are *in relation* to the other terms respectively" (BISHOP COPLESTON). "A remarkable example of this kind", adds Copleston, "is that argument of Toplady against free-will, who, after quoting the text, *Ye also as lively stones are built up in a spiritual house*, triumphantly exclaims: 'this is giving free-will a stab under the fifth rib; for can stones hew themselves and build themselves in a regular house?' "

The *likeness* existing between things whose resemblance is likely to prove rhetorically effective— *e.g.* a galleon and a castle, the public mind and the rising tide—exists therefore only in respect of certain definite qualities or relations common to both. "When Apollo, running after Daphne," says Johnson, "is likened to a greyhound chasing a hare, there is nothing gained; the ideas of pursuit and flight are too plain to be made plainer." That is true; but a further objection might be urged on the plea, that the things are *essentially alike*, that there is a resemblance *in kind*. Although, when the figure is intended for didactic effect, a very close likeness is possible; a truly rhetorical resemblance seldom or never amounts to a resemblance *in kind*. Care must consequently be had that only common qualities or relations be referred to, or implied, in the figure.

The hill in *Treasure Island* called Spy-glass "was likewise the strangest in configuration, running up sheer from almost every side, and then suddenly cut off at the top like a *pedestal* to put a statue on".

In this *didactic* figure the intrinsic resemblance is as close as it well may be; there is still a difference in kind.

"I remember his breath *hanging like smoke*, in his wake, as he strode off."

Ditto.

"sand *dancing* in the spring at the bottom of the kettle, for all the world like *porridge* beginning to boil."

Ditto.

"Mutiny, it was plain, hung over us like a *thundercloud*."

An *emotional* figure; a very marked difference in kind.

Simile and Metaphor. When this *likeness* is explicitly stated, and two distinct pictures are deliberately presented to the mind, the writer makes use of the rhetorical figure called *Simile*.

"built high like castles." "the whole ship creaking, groaning, and jumping like a manufactory."	Depending upon similarity.

When, on account of an easily recognizable likeness, the name of one thing is transferred to the other, and the one thing is spoken of in terms of the other, the figure is called *Metaphor*.

"those great Spanish *castles.*"	Meaning 'galleons' (similarity).
"the *long-eared* race of his critics."	By reason of similarity (the possession of one or more qualities in common).
"that now he was The ivy, which had hid my princely trunk, And sucked my verdure out on't" [Prospero speaking of his brother Antonio, *Tempest*, i. 2].	By virtue of an analogy: *Antonio* : Prospero :: *ivy* : trunk. Antonio is spoken of in terms of 'ivy'.
"the *eye* of the soul."	Meaning reason (analogy).
"keen *arrowy* rhetoric."	Analogy. *rhetoric* : its object :: *arrow* : its object.
"who was the first lion-hearted man that ventured to *make sail* in this *frail boat* of prose."	Analogy.
"partly from the *damping* influence of this alarm."	'alarm' is spoken of in terms of 'water' by reason of similar action upon the same thing. *alarm* : x :: *water* : x.

I. THE SIMILE.

Construction of Simile. There are four methods of constructing a *simile*: (1) we may deliberately connect the two pictures; (2) we may present them separately without connectives; (3) we may develop part of the picture separately; (4) we may state the resemblance, and then develop the picture.

(1) When the two ideas are quickly expressed, it is always well to use connectives: as . . . so; like, &c.; *e.g.*:

"To omit all italics in English is like removing the direction-posts to remedy the intricacies of a road"; or,

"To omit all italics in English is no less absurd than to attempt to remedy the intricacies of a road by removing the direction-posts".

(2) When the pictures are not quickly developed; that is, when either side of the comparison is elaborate, it is well to omit connectives; *e.g.*:

Campbell on antithesis: "the excess itself into which some writers have fallen is an evidence of its value—of the lustre and emphasis which antithesis is calculated to give to the expression. *There is no risk of intemperance in using a liquor which has neither spirit nor flavour.*"

But observe the following:

"For, as the bee that gathereth honey out of the weed, when she espieth the fair flower flieth to the sweetest; or, as the kind spaniel, though he hunt after birds, yet forsakes them to retrieve the partridge; or, as we commonly feed on beef hungerly at the first, yet, seeing the quail more dainty, change our diet; so I, though I loved Philautus for his good properties, yet, seeing Euphues to excel him, I ought by nature to love him better".

Here, there are at least two faults: (*a*) the cumulation of similes—for prose purposes *one* of the above would have been quite sufficient; (*b*) the abuse of connectives. Write:

"*The bee, that gathereth honey out of the weed, when she espieth the fair flower flieth to the sweetest.* Though I loved Philautus for his good properties, yet, seeing Euphues to excel him, I ought by nature to love him better."

Contrast:

"Thus, as the torpedo, when it feels itself ensnared by the deceitful hook, vomits forth a baneful humour into the briny ocean, and not only fills the places near adjoining to her with a chilling ice, but sends it up to the angler's hand, wherewith in a moment it benumbs and charms his senses into a death-resembling sleep: so Periander's sorrow entangled with love's bait, &c." (CROWNE's *Pandion and Amphigenia*).

"We are told of *the torpedo, that it has the wonderful quality of numbing everything it touches*. A paraphrase is like a torpedo; by its influence," &c. (CAMPBELL's *Rhetoric*).

By means of such a construction as Dr. Campbell here adopts, he might have introduced just as much detail as Crowne, without endangering the sense of the passage or the sanity of the reader.

(3) A resemblance is powerful only when the perception of it is *flashed* upon the reader's mind. Dr. Whately should have recognized this, yet, speaking of Johnson's imitators, he writes:

"They bear the same resemblance to their model that the armour of the Chinese, *as described by travellers, consisting of thick quilted cotton covered with stiff glazed paper*, does to that of the ancient knights, equally glittering and bulky, but destitute of the temper and firmness which was its sole advantage".

In order that a simile may be effective, we should see it suddenly, and see it whole. The total impression from Whately's simile is delayed by the phrase:

"*as described by travellers, consisting of thick quilted cotton covered with stiff glazed paper*".

This detail should therefore be either omitted altogether, or stated separately. Omit it altogether, and observe how much more vivid the picture becomes:

"They bear the same resemblance to their model that the armour of the Chinese does to that of the ancient knights, equally glittering and bulky, but destitute of that temper and firmness which was its sole advantage".

Dr. Whately probably considered the detail essential to the picture. He should, in such case, have developed that part of the picture separately thus:

"The armour of the Chinese, travellers tell us, consists of thick quilted cotton covered with stiff glazed paper. The writings of Johnson's imitators appear to bear the same resemblance to their model as this Chinese armour does to that of the ancient knights, equally glittering and bulky, but destitute of the temper and firmness which was its sole advantage."

In this case, the simile is foreshadowed by a little preliminary picture.

(4) Lastly, the simile may first be stated; after which the writer may proceed to develop his picture separately.

"We have often thought that the motion of the public mind in our country resembles that of the sea, when the tide is rising. Each successive wave rushes forward, breaks, and rolls back; but the great flood is steadily coming in. A person who looked on the waters only for a moment might fancy that they were retiring, or that they obeyed no fixed law, but were rushing capriciously to and fro. But, when he keeps his eye on them for a quarter of an hour, and sees one sea-mark disappear after another, it is impossible for him to doubt of the general direction in which the ocean is moved. Just such has been the course of events in England."

Observe how every detail in this picture of the advancing tide—the successive waves breaking and rolling back, the spectator thinking they were retiring, the sea-marks disappearing—is in exact keeping with the subject to be illustrated, the progress of the national mind. The analogy is never for an instant marred by any feature of unlikeness. The writer has taken care to refer only to those relations common alike to *the public mind* and *the rising tide*.

II. THE METAPHOR.

Nature of Metaphor. In the Simile we call up a resemblance between two things; in the *Metaphor* we identify two things, and speak of one in the terms that belong to the other.

"His song is too much ballasted with prose."

We are writing of a song, as if it were a ship; a ship and a song are identified.

A perfect metaphor is of course always capable of being expanded into a simile, being in fact a simile condensed. But a metaphor, if the resemblance may be readily caught, is in general preferable to a simile. Most metaphors would be greatly weakened by expansion into simile. In other words, an implied resemblance is generally more effective than an explicit statement of such resemblance; "because", as Dr. Whately says, "all men are more gratified at catching the resemblance for themselves, than at having it pointed out to them". "And, accordingly," he adds, "the greatest masters of this kind of style, when the case will not admit of pure metaphor, generally prefer a mixture of metaphor with simile, first pointing out the similitude, and afterwards employing metaphorical terms which imply it; or, *vice versâ*, explaining a metaphor by a statement of the comparison" (see page 140).

Liability to confuse literal words with figurative. The construction of the Metaphor requires that the phrase should be *proper to the figure*. We must not combine literal terms with figurative. Thus we may speak of an author's style as "feeble"; the word has become as literal in its application to "style" as to "person". We cannot, however, speak of the "*feebleness* of style produced by excessive dilution": a spirit is rendered by dilution not "feeble" but "weak"; and, since we are speaking metaphorically, *i.e.* speaking of "style" in such terms as belong to "spirit", we should say: "the *weakness* of style produced by excessive dilution".

In the following examples, the literal words that clash with the figurative are italicised:

"He is a shallow stream, *fretting and fuming* at every stone" [a shallow-minded man, finding an obstacle in everything.]　*fretting and fuming* are literal terms applying to "he" and cannot be used of "stream".

"The echoes of his *overheated* language have faded away."　an *echo* suggests "sound" not "heat".

"chalk of various colours with which the *tame* thoughts had submitted to be rubbed over in order to be made fine."　We may rub a *coarse* substance, but not a "tame" substance "fine".

"The *outline* of his life may be *gathered* from . . ."　"may be *drawn* from."

"*intercourse* with the source of all beauty."　We may have *knowledge* of a source, but not "intercourse" with it.

"he *based* his writings on artistic lines."　*designed.*

"It is pretty clear that Herodotus stood, and meant to stand, on that isthmus between the regions of poetry and blank *unimpassioned* prose."　*unimpassioned* mars the geographical picture; try desolate: "blank, desolate prose".

Contrast with the above that phrase of Burke's, so perfect in its *metaphorical truth*:

France has "the honour of *leading up* the death-*dance* of democratic revolution".

Or this of De Quincey's:

"But when both were gone, it may be truly affirmed that the great *oracles* of rhetoric were finally *silenced*".

Or this of Ben Jonson's:

"gently *stir* the *mould* about the *root* of the question".

"Words which, by long use in a transferred sense," writes Archbishop Whately, "have lost nearly all their metaphorical force may fairly be combined in a manner which, taking them literally, would be incongruous. It would savour of hyper-criticism to object to such an expression as 'fertile source'". The whole of our abstract vocabulary consists indeed of words used in such a transferred sense: thus *spirit* is no longer 'breath', nor do we actually 'lay hold on', when we *apprehend*, nor 'build up', when we *edify*. Language is full of *tropes* (*i.e.* single words employed in a transferred sense), because no language is so copious as to have one word appropriated to every idea; a word will consequently signify some definite idea, and also those ideas which are analogous or similar to the original. Thus words may become 'proper' terms in many transferred senses; and in using them we never think of their literal application, this being rather of etymological than rhetorical interest.

Nevertheless there are words that still remain, as Blair says, "in a sort of middle state". He justly insists that in the use of such words, correctness often demands "a regard to the figure and allusion on which they are founded". For example, the term "vein" as in a " vein of thought" has been so long used in a transferred sense as to become in that transferred sense almost a proper term. Yet, if we speak of "excelling in a certain vein of thought" we mar the original figure; better therefore "some writers have one vein that is peculiarly excellent" than "in which they peculiarly excel". What a perfect image may be constructed even out of a 'proper' term like "vein", by associating with it such words as restore its original meaning, may be seen in the following sentence:

"Daniel Defoe then proceeded to *work* the *vein* which was *opened* by ' Robinson Crusoe ' ".

The epithet "dead letter" is in such a middle state; the following sentence is consequently to be censured for confusion of figure:

"Comic opera, for a long time *a dead letter*, has at length *raised its head* from the dust ".

As also:

"This *opens up* serious *food* for reflection ".	The word *food* has somewhat of its original meaning still clinging to it, and should therefore be associated with *supplies* or *provides*.
" *Contact* with a bad social atmosphere."	say ' *breathing* a . . .'

"One may be", says Dr. Blair, "'sheltered under the patronage of a great man', but it were wrong to say, 'sheltered under the mask of dissimulation', as a mask conceals but does not shelter. An object, in description, may be 'clothed', if you will, with 'epithets', but it is not proper to speak of its being

'clothed with circumstances', as the word 'circumstances' alludes to standing round, not to cloth-
ing. Such attentions as these to the propriety of
language are required in every composition." It
is, indeed, this close attention to the figurative
value (*i.e.* the etymology) of words, that displays
them in their true colour.

Confusion of Metaphor. It often happens that the phrases
we use are faulty, not because they
are literal, but because they belong to different
figures. It is so natural an operation to find images
for our thoughts, that the pictures tend often to
crowd one upon another, and produce a *confusion
of metaphor.*

"A much more brilliant writer, though a less *minute anatomist of ebbs and flows and cross-currents* of feeling, was Richardson's great successor and caricaturist, Henry Fielding."	One cannot *anatomise* the *tides*; one may only *observe* and *reason* about them. Two metaphors are mixed. Say either "an anatomist of passion and feeling", or "an observer of the ebbs and flows and cross-currents of feeling".
"Mr. —— has *unearthed* a real *star.*"	"Turnips" may be *unearthed,* but not "stars".

A single word belonging to another picture will
often cause confusion in the figure:

"It is nothing but an endeavour on the part of *crumbling* and decrepit England to seek shelter under the arm of Uncle Sam".	The image is that of a weak or "decrepit" man, seeking shelter under the arm of a stronger neighbour. The word *crumbling* belongs to quite another picture, *e.g.* an old house. A man, be he ever so "decrepit", will never "crumble".

For absolute accuracy of figure, each single sentence should be devoted to a single picture. This

picture may, of course, be elaborated in another sentence, so it pass not beyond the limits of resemblance:

"St. Austin, in his Confessions, and wherever he becomes peculiarly interesting, is apt to be impassioned and fervent in a degree, which makes him *break out of the proper pace* of rhetoric. *He is matched to trot, and is continually breaking out into a gallop.*"

But two different images should not be presented in the same sentence:

"Art and Nature go [1] hand in hand; and it is well nigh impossible to say where [2] Art ends and Nature begins.	The second figure coming on the heels of the first suggests a ludicrous entanglement.
"Nature and Art [1] must walk then hand in hand, [2] the one giving force and originality, the other beauty and polish."	A similar clash of figure.
"But, as we may see more than once in the history of our prose, false ornament, however distasteful, is, on the whole, a better and more healthy sign than no ornament at all; a prose style which [1] *moves too timidly,* and [2] *fears all that is gorgeous* lest it become tawdry, and all that is strenuous lest it become exaggerated, soon becomes [1] *afraid of its own shadow, and ceases to move at all.*"	There is a confusion here (although the metaphors are not intervolved) between,[1] a person moving timidly and fearful of his shadow, and,[2] a person fearful of elaborate dress. One of these images should suffice.
"His artistic powers are [1] *crushed,* perhaps [2] *vanish completely.*"	The second image is again inconsonant with the first. Say: "perhaps completely destroyed".
"The mind, [1] *running into a by-way,* and [2] *engrossed in the whirl of pleasure.*"	Here again two images tumble the one over the other.

Contrast with these confused pictures, the perfect images presented in the following sentences:

"Now, if these men have defeated the law, and *outrun* native punishment, though they can *outstrip* men, they have *no wings* to *fly* from God".

"The biographer, especially of a literary man, need only mark the *main currents* of tendency, without being officious to trace out to its *marshy source* every *runlet* that has cast in its tiny pitcherful with the rest."

"For the consequence of sentences, you must be sure that every clause do give *the cue* one to the other, and be *bespoken* ere it come."

Length of Metaphor. It is not possible to speak for a long time with propriety of one thing in terms of something else. The metaphor consequently does not allow of such expansion as the simile. Indeed, to dilate a metaphor beyond a single sentence generally carries it beyond the points at which identity exists. We must "not presume that because the relation is the same or similar in one or two points, therefore it is the same or similar in all" (COPLESTON).

The old author of the *Ancren Riwle*, it may be remembered, successfully established an analogy between Christ, wooing Mansoul, and a far king, wooing a distressed princess:

"This king is Christ, who came wooing our soul, which the devils had beset: He sent his prophets, and at length He came himself".

Up to this point, the relationship is identical, and a metaphorical transference would be possible. But remark how the author proceeds:

"He put him in tourney, and, for love of his lady, like a brave knight, had in the fight his shield pierced on every side. This shield that concealed His divinity was His dear body that was spread on the Cross, broad as a shield above at His outstretched arms, and narrow beneath, where one foot rested on the other. That His shield had no side is in token that His disciples who should have stood by Him and been His sides, fled away from Him, and left Him as they would a stranger, &c."

Below is written:

"In a shield there are three things: the wood, the leather, and the painting. Just so was it in this shield: the wood of the Cross, and the leather of the body of the Lord, and the painting of the red blood that covered it so fair."

Combination of Simile and Metaphor. "The highest intellects are the first to catch and to reflect the dawn." An identity is here established between "high intellects" and the "tops of mountains"; and terms proper to mountain-tops are used figuratively of intellects. The perception of such an identity as this is often assisted by supplementing the metaphor with a simile, thus:

"The highest intellects, *like the tops of mountains*, are the first to catch and to reflect the dawn".

Compare Pope's—

"Which, *like a wounded snake*, drags its slow length along",

and Walter Scott's—

"In the meanwhile, the more distinguished persons of each train followed their patrons into the lofty halls and ante-chambers of the royal palace, flowing on in the same current, *like two streams which are compelled into the same channel*, yet shun to mix their waters".

Again, in the following:

"It lay in those accidents of time and place which obliged Greece to spin most of her speculations out of her own bowels", it is not instantly clear with what Greece is identified; accordingly, De Quincey did well in writing:

> "to spin most of her speculations, *like a spider*, out of her own bowels".

Personal Metaphor and Personification. A special kind of transference is that whereby we attribute animate action to inanimate objects or ideas— *Personal Metaphor*. The action may be analogous, or merely the effect of the action may be analogous; *e.g.*:

> *laughing* stream; *smiling* prospect; *sombre* day; a *night of tears*; the *babbling* brook; the *sighing* wind; *whispering* trees; the *anger* of the storm; *glowing* eloquence; *stony* heart; "The gunwale was *lipping* astern"; "The ship was *talking*, as sailors say".

The difference between a *Personal Metaphor* and a *Personification* is one of degree only. When we assert the transferred attributes as *literally true* of the object, we have developed the Personal Metaphor into a *Personification*; *e.g.*:

> "The morning light was in no hurry to climb the prison-wall, and look in at the snuggery window".
>
> "Seeing the day begin to disclose her comfortable beauties."
>
> "The ship was . . . treading the innumerable ripples with an incessant weltering splash."

Carlyle is full of Personifications: *the Destinies, the Necessities, the dumb Veracities, the Eternal Voices, Fact, Nature*: a man who bends to circumstances is "loyal to Fact"; a man who does not realize the inevitability of, say, democracy, is "disloyal to Fact".

"All poetry," says Dr. Blair, "even in its most

gentle and humble forms, abounds with it [*Personal Metaphor and Personification*]. From prose it is far from being excluded; nay, in common conversation, very frequent approaches are made to it. When we say the ground *thirsts* for rain, or the earth *smiles* with plenty; when we speak of ambitions being *restless*, or a disease being *deceitful*, such expressions show the facility with which the mind can accommodate the properties of living creatures to things that are inanimate, or to abstract conceptions of its own forming."

III. THE USE OF FIGURED PROSE.

Figurative Thought. De Quincey objects against John Foster, the essayist, that "the imagery and ornamental parts of his Essays have evidently not grown up in the loom, and concurrently with the texture of the thoughts, but have been separately added afterwards as so much embroidery or fringe". If a resemblance does not spontaneously suggest itself, it will never weld with the expression. We must think in our figures, if we are to write a figured style. Purple shreds sewn on to a thought, which is in itself neither inspiring nor imaginative, are worse in their effect than new patches on an old coat. We should remember that, "when the ornaments cost labour, that labour always appears". The small number of figures that Stevenson found it necessary to employ in writing the most picturesque passages of his *Treasure Island* is quite remarkable. It is only when a lively resemblance forces itself upon him, that he troubles to set it down. "Nothing derogates more from the weight and dignity of any composition than too great attention to ornament."

"Let us satisfy ourselves," says Blair, "by considering that without this talent [for figurative language], or at least with a very small measure of it, we may both write and speak to advantage. Good sense, clear ideas, perspicuity of language, and proper arrangement of words and thoughts will always command attention. These are indeed the foundations of all solid merit, both in speaking and writing. Many subjects require nothing more; and those which admit of ornament admit it only as a secondary requisite. To study and to know our own genius well; to follow nature; to seek to improve, but not to force it—are directions which cannot be too often given to those who desire to excel in the liberal arts."

Propriety of Figures. Take care that the image is strictly appropriate to the thought. The picture presented (1) should not mislead, (2) should not degrade, (3) neither should it be too elevated in its character.

(1) A misleading image is presented in the following: "imagination *forms an outlet for* the other gifts of nature"; imagination may indeed be said *to assist in their display.*

(2) The following metaphor of De Quincey's is below the dignity of his subject:

"Burton is too quaint, fantastic, and disjointed; Milton is too solemn and continuous. In the one we see the flutter of a para-

chute; in the other, the stately and voluminous gyrations of an ascending *balloon*."

Below, however, there is a *humorous* propriety, when De Quincey says of the prose of Milton, that he "*polonaises* with a grand Castilian air", and a proper dignity in the implied comparison: "his thoughts and his imagery still appear to move to the music of the organ ".

The figure, "supernatural corns", in the following is meaningless and vulgar:

"He was one of those many wayfarers on the road of life, who seem to be afflicted with *supernatural corns*, rendering it impossible for them to keep up even with their lame competitors ".

It is difficult to remain on an elevated plane of thought with such supports as: "the world wiping its eyes on its great pocket-handkerchief ", or "eagle-eyed Jack Horners picking the plums out of the books of the season " [*critics*].

It was a degrading image of this kind in Masson's *Life of Milton* that provoked the following criticism from Russell Lowell:

"Discussing the motives of Milton's first marriage, he (Masson) says, 'Did he come seeking his £500, and did Mrs. Powell *heave a daughter at him*?' We have heard of a woman throwing herself at a man's head, and the image is a somewhat violent one; but what is this to Mr. Masson's improvement on it? It has been sometimes affirmed that the fitness of an image may be tested by trying whether a picture could be made of it or not. Mr. Masson has certainly offered a new and striking subject to the historical school of British art."

(3) Nothing should be elevated above its degree (or degraded below it) except for emotional or

humorous effect. In either case we must take care that the image is *essentially true*. As far as concerns prose, *Hyperboles* have generally a humorous purpose; they are justifiable when there is no outrage to the reader's sense of truth.

" blow through his nose like a foghorn."

" thus it happens that such a thing as a long or an involved sentence can hardly be produced from French literature, though a sultan were to offer his daughter in marriage to the man who should find it."

" our modern sentences agitate us by rolling fires after the fashion of those internal earthquakes, that, not content with one throe, run along spasmodically in a long succession of intermitting convulsions."

"As it were." "It is", says Blair, " but a bad and ungraceful softening, which writers sometimes use for a harsh metaphor, when they palliate it with the expression, *as it were*. This is but an awkward parenthesis; and metaphors which need this apology of an *as it were* would generally have been better omitted."

IV. EPITHETS.

Propriety of Epithets. In a metaphor we transfer the name of one thing to something else on the ground of an analogy or a similarity existing between them; in an *Epithet* we transfer the name of a part to the whole, or of the whole to a part, or we name a thing by some aspect or concomitant circumstance. The proseman is concerned with two types of Epithet:

(1) Synecdoche,
(2) Metonymy,

in regard to which he is to observe much the same laws as he does in the case of the metaphor; *i.e.* he must preserve an exact correspondence between the epithet and the spirit of the sentence.

For example, naming the whole by a part (Synecdoche), we might use for Dr. Johnson the epithet "great lexicographer"; the epithet, if used, must be consonant with the spirit of the thought. Suppose, for instance, we say, "the great lexicographer was very sparing in his use of rhetorical figures", the epithet is not justified, because the fact of Johnson's being a lexicographer has no particular bearing upon the rest of the sentence, "is very sparing in his use of rhetorical figures". If, however, we say, "the great lexicographer, who must have been painfully aware of the deficiencies of the vocabulary, exercised a severe restraint in the coining and addition of words"—the epithet is justified, because it is closely associated with the spirit of the sentence.

Again, naming the whole by a significant part (Synecdoche), we may refer to the crew of a ship as 'hands'. If we wish to preserve the image, and not to convert 'hands' into a proper term, we shall refrain from such expressions as "the hands were about to remark", or "the hands thought"; whereas "the hands were ready", "the hands were willing", will be found *figuratively proper*.

There are large numbers of *epithets*, as of metaphors, which are scarcely distinguishable from 'proper' terms. But even when they have become proper terms, a recognition of their exact figurative value frequently enables the writer to give an added colour to his style. By associating them with phrases that are proper to them in their original meaning, a pictorial value is imparted to the sentence. I append, therefore, a brief summary of the various kinds of Synecdoche and Metonymy that may occur in prose.

Synecdoche. SYNECDOCHE: *a transference of the name of the part to the whole.* We may render an impression more telling and picturesque by charging the mind exclusively with some commanding particular or efficient point.

THE PART.	THE WHOLE.
"blade and edge."	sword.
"point and edge" (O.E. *ord and ecy*).	
"hands."	sailors, &c.
(*willing hands make light work.*)	
"the great lexicographer."	Johnson.
"the conqueror of Jena."	Napoleon.

Other varieties of this transference are:

(*a*) *Species for Genus.*—Again, we have a special term producing a picturesque effect, because it chains the mind to a definite image:

THE SPECIES.	THE GENUS.
"bread."	food.
(*Give us this day our daily bread.*)	
"lilies of the field."	flowers.
(*Consider the lilies of the field.*)	
"a Cræsus", "a Shakespeare", "a Demosthenes", "a Cromwell", "some village Hampden."	a rich man, a great poet, an orator, a democrat, a patriot.

Occasionally it will be found that, contrary to

principle, the whole will be found more picturesque than the part, the genus more broadly suggestive than the species. For this reason, and also for *euphemism* (*i.e.* to obscure rather than to enlighten) we find genus substituted for species:

THE GENUS.	THE SPECIES.
" the plain."	field of battle.
" departed."	dead.
" liquor."	strong drink.
" the vessel."	the ship.
"*silver and gold* have I none."	money.
" the steel."	sword.

(*b*) *Abstract for Concrete.*—We dilate some quality or characteristic until we identify it with the possessor, and speak of it in concrete terms.

THE ABSTRACT (the part).	THE CONCRETE (the whole).
" youth is young, youth is hopeful, age despondent."	the young man; the old man.
"ambition may not be checked so."	the ambitious man.
"old honesty was there."	honest man.

We may also substitute the concrete for the abstract: 'fool' for 'folly', 'knave' for 'knavery'.

(*c*) *The possessor for the thing possessed.*

e.g. " ye devour the *families* of widows ".

Metonymy. METONYMY: *naming a thing by some concomitant circumstance or incidental aspect.* Again, a special and suggestive image is thrown on the mind.

THE CIRCUMSTANCE OR ASPECT.	THE FACT OR THING.
"They would never incur the risk of seeing an invading army encamped between Utrecht and Amsterdam."	They would not run the risk of invasion.
"she of the seven hills."	Rome.
"the all-hiding earth had received him."	he was dead.
"passes to his unknown home."	
"brought his *grey hairs* in sorrow to the grave."	the old man.

The following varieties of metonymy should be noticed:

(*a*) The name of the instrument is transferred to the agent:

INSTRUMENT.	AGENT.
"The *pen* is mightier than the *sword*".	the writer, the fighter.
"This is the production of a ready *pen*."	
"The *pulpit* hurled its thunders."	the preacher.
"With *fire* and *sword*."	an army burning and slaying.

(*b*) The symbol for the office, or the person holding office:

SYMBOL.	OFFICE OR OFFICIAL.
"Town and *gown* rows".	University undergraduates.
"The *mitre* was all-powerful."	the bishop.
"He ascended the *throne*."	became king.
"The *crown* became him well."	the kingly office.
"The *laurel*."	fame.

(*c*) The passion for the object of passion, the gift for the giver, &c.:

"The lord is my *song*".	object of song.
"He is become my *salvation*."	giver of salvation.
"My *aversion*, my *love*, my *joy*."	object of aversion, love, joy.

(*d*) Inventor for invention, effect for cause, container for contained, &c.:

"Bacchus"; a "Bunsen".	wine; a kind of burner (inventor for invention).
"His *blood* be upon your hands."	death (effect for cause).
"the *cup* that cheers." "addicted to the *bottle*." "power of the *purse*." "set the *table* in a roar."	Container for thing contained.

In regard to all these varieties of Epithet it is necessary to exercise a care equal to that observed in the use of the Metaphor. See that the expression (whether a figure of contiguity, of contrast, of analogy, or of similarity) be coincident with the bent of the imagination.

Finally, in regard to all Figures of Prose, it should be remembered, that the prose-ideal is an ideal not of pleasure but of power. It was this *ideal of power* that Ben Jonson had in mind, when he wrote: "he never forced his language, nor went out of the highway of speaking, but for some great necessity, or apparent profit; for he denied figures to be invented for ornament, but for aid".

INDEX.

Adjective, Inversion of, 48, 52–54; Order of, 52, 53.
Adjective-clause, Continuating and Restrictive, 28, 34, 57–60; Co-ordination of, 61–63; Reference of, 55–57; Sequence of, 60, 61.
Adjective Group, Order of, 53, 54.
Adverb, Correlative, 42; Order of, 38–45; Relative Value of, 43.
Adverb-clause, Order of, 45–48.
Adverb-phrase, in front-position, 43–45; Order of, 38–45.
Analogy, 123, 124.
"As it were", 143.

Balance, Crossed, 86, 87; Defect of, 85; in Sentence, 84–87.
Blair's Rules for Sentence-unity, 31–36.

Choice of Words, 13–15, 21–27.
Clearness, 24, 25.
Colloquialism, 21, 22.
Colon, Uses of, 74–76.
Comma, Uses of, 66–73.
Copula in Paragraph, 105–107, et seq.
Crossed Balance, 86, 87.

Dash, Uses of, 78, 79.
Descriptive Paragraph, 94–97, 114–116.

Epithets, Nature of, 143; Propriety of, 144.
Exactness in Speech, 21–23.

Figure, Confusion of, 135–137; Confusion of literal words with figurative, 131–135; Difference between rhetorical figure and concrete example, 124–126; Figurative Thought, 140, 141; Propriety of, 141–143; Prose-ideal of, 148.
Fixed Order, Rules of, 37.
Full-stop, Uses of, 76.

Harmony, 25, 26.

Insincerity in Diction, 12-15.
Intermediate Paragraph, 92-94
Introductory Paragraph, 91, 92.
Inversion: of Object, 52; of Predicate Word, 51; of Subject and
  Predicate, 49-51; Reasons of, 48, 49.

Loose-resolved Sentence, 83, 84.
Loose Sentence, 81-84.

Metaphor, 127, 131-139; combined with Simile, 138, 139; Confusion
  of figure, 135-137; Confusion of literal words with figurative,
  131-135; Length of, 137, 138; Nature of, 131; Personal Metaphor, 139, 140.
Metonymy, 146-148.

Note of Exclamation, Uses of, 77, 78.
Note of Interrogation, Uses of, 77.

"Only", "merely", "not", &c., 41, 42.
Order of Words, 36-65.

Paragraph, Descriptive, 94-97, 114-116; Discipline of, 87-91;
  Intermediate, 92-94; Introductory, 91, 92; Paragraph of Sum-
  mary, 97, 113; Predicative, 97-113, 116-122; Subject of Para-
  graph, Rules for, 105; Topic of Paragraph, 98-105; Unity of
  Paragraph, 87-91.
Paragraph-close, 105, 106, 109, *et seq.*
Paragraph-copula, 105-107, *et seq.*
Paragraph-glide, 101-103.
Paragraph-subject, Rules for, 105.
Paragraph-topic, first sentence, 103-105; Introduction of, 98-101;
  Place of 98-101.
Paragraph-types, 91-122.
Participial Phrase, 64, 65.
Periodic Sentence, 81-84.
Period-stop, Uses of, 76.
Personal Metaphor, 139, 140.
Personification, 139, 140.
Pleonasm, 20.
Predicative Paragraph, 97-113, 116-122.

Pronoun, Explicit Reference of, 54, 55; Relative, Omission of, 64; Relative, Use of, 57–63.
Punctuation, 66–79.

Rapidity of Style, 64, 65.
Reading, Reflective, 7–9.
Reference of Pronoun, 54, 55; of Adjective-clause, 55–57.
Relative Pronoun, Omission of, 64; Use of, 57–63.
Relative Words and Clauses, 54–63.
Resolution of the Sentence, 80, 81, 83, 84.
Rules, Necessity of, 9–11.

Semi-colon, Uses of, 73, 74.
Sentence, Balanced Form, 84–86; Balanced Order, 86, 87; Co-ordinate Elements of, 29–31; Length of, 79–81; Loose Sentence, 81-84; Loose-resolved Sentence, 83, 84; Nature of Sentences, 79–87; Periodic Sentence, 81–84; Resolution of Sentence, 80, 81, 83, 84; Structure of Sentence, 36–65; Unity of Sentence, 27–36.
Sentence-glide, 45, 49, 52, 54.
Similarity, 123, 124.
Simile, Construction of, 127–130; Definition of, 127; Simile combined with Metaphor, 138, 139.
Simplicity, 23, 24.
Stops, Use of, 66–79.
Synecdoche, 145, 146.
Synonym, 15–17.

Tautology, 15–19.
"That", Use of, 57–63.

Unity in the Paragraph, 87–91; in the Sentence, 27–36.

"Which", Use of, 57–63.
"Who", Use of, 57–63.
Words, Choice of, 13–15, 21–27; Grammatical Order of, 36–48; Knowledge of, 11, 12; Rhetorical Order of, 48–65.

www.ingramcontent.com/pod-product-compliance
Lightning Source LLC
Chambersburg PA
CBHW021129020726
47500CB00003B/998